GIBSONS & D
BOX 109, GI

D0341692

PRISONER of ICE and SNOW

RUTH LAUREN

BLOOMSBURY

NEW YORK   LONDON   OXFORD   NEW DELHI   SYDNEY

Copyright © 2017 by Ruth Lauren
All rights reserved. No part of this book may be reproduced or transmitted in any form
or by any means, electronic or mechanical, including photocopying, recording, or by any
information storage and retrieval system, without permission in writing from the publisher.

First published in the United States of America in April 2017
by Bloomsbury Children's Books
www.bloomsbury.com

Bloomsbury is a registered trademark of Bloomsbury Publishing Plc

For information about permission to reproduce selections from this book, write to
Permissions, Bloomsbury Children's Books, 1385 Broadway, New York, New York 10018
Bloomsbury books may be purchased for business or promotional use. For information
on bulk purchases please contact Macmillan Corporate and Premium Sales Department at
specialmarkets@macmillan.com

Library of Congress Cataloging-in-Publication Data
Names: Lauren, Ruth, author.
Title: Prisoner of ice and snow / by Ruth Lauren.
Description: New York : Bloomsbury, April 2017.
Summary: When thirteen-year-old Valor is arrested, she could not be happier. Demidova's
prison for criminal children is exactly where she wants to be. Valor's sister, Sasha,
is already serving a life sentence for stealing from the royal family, and Valor is
going to help her escape . . . from the inside.
Identifiers: LCCN 2016025579 (print) • LCCN 2016045172 (e-book)
ISBN 978-1-68119-131-7 (hardcover) • ISBN 978-1-68119-132-4 (e-book)
Subjects: | CYAC: Sisters—Fiction. | Prisons—Fiction. | Fantasy. | BISAC: JUVENILE FICTION
/ Fantasy & Magic. | JUVENILE FICTION / Action & Adventure / Survival Stories. | JUVENILE
FICTION / Family / Siblings.
Classification: LCC PZ7.1.L3816 Pr 2017 (print) | LCC PZ7.1.L3816 (e-book) | DDC [Fic]—dc23
LC record available at https://lccn.loc.gov/2016025579

Book design by Colleen Andrews
Typeset by Newgen Knowledge Works (P) Ltd., Chennai, India
Printed and bound in the U.S.A. by Berryville Graphics Inc., Berryville, Virginia
2 4 6 8 10 9 7 5 3 1

All papers used by Bloomsbury Publishing, Inc., are natural, recyclable products
made from wood grown in well-managed forests. The manufacturing processes
conform to the environmental regulations of the country of origin.

For Lauren

CHAPTER 1

"Valor!"

I ignore my name, called from behind me, and slide faster through the crowd, releasing the earflaps on my *ushanka* to hide my face. I'm almost running by the time she catches me.

"Valor."

Mother plucks at my sleeve, snagging my arm, and I have to stop and face her. Her hands are gloved in the blue-tinged white fur of a winter hare, her cheeks pinched pink by the bitter cold. There are lines around her dark eyes, shadows under them that weren't there a month ago.

"Didn't you hear me?" She tugs on one of the leather laces dangling from my hat.

I scuff my boot over the snow packed between the cobbles and try not to look up at the clock tower. I don't have time for this now.

"Where are you going? Your father and I think it would be better if you stayed close," she says, gesturing at the crowds filling the square. Market vendors trundle their carts along, wafting the smell of hot cocoa and roasted chestnuts into the air. Peasants and nobility alike mill around us, all looking for the perfect viewing spot for the royal parade. They won't find it. I already have it marked out for myself.

I force a smile, though she's probably not expecting it. It's been decreed that every one of the queen's subjects attend today—even my parents, who are in disgrace, banished to our estate outside the city. "I'm only looking for a better place to stand. Today will go down in the records of the great library as a historic one for the realm."

She nods, though I'm simply parroting what my father said yesterday. I try not to think about the discussion, about Father still trying to put the good of the realm first no matter how much pain it causes him. I can't afford to get distracted now.

"Mother, please, I just want to see the ceremony."

She blinks the hoarfrost from lashes as long and dark as my own, weighing up whether she should agree.

The cobbles are cold under my boots, even through the two layers of fleece lining them. I open my mouth to say something, anything that will excuse me from standing at my parents' sides when I need to be elsewhere, but Mother does it for me, reaching out to touch my arm. Neither of us can feel it through layers of heavy embroidered dresses and coats, but it doesn't matter.

"You're right. You've done nothing wrong, and here I am acting as though you have."

I'm not used to hearing my mother be so uncertain of herself. She shouldn't have to be here like this after the shock of what my sister has done. She doesn't even look the same, stripped of the gray furs that signify a royal official's position.

"Find us again when—"

"I'm quite safe with the whole Guard out in force. This is . . . it's important to me." My chest aches from lying to her like this, but I can't let anything stand in my way.

A cry of delight goes through the crowd as the first ice sculpture is unveiled on the palace steps. It's a dancer, her sparkling arms outstretched, her body flung from a giant open palm behind her as if she has exploded from it. She's caught in mid-movement, her legs arced gracefully and her hair spilling in frozen liquid waves as if moving to music we can't hear.

The palace rises up behind her, glittering in the morning light, its towers and bright domes cutting into a snow-white sky. Barriers have been erected to form a pathway from one end of the huge square to the other. They lead right from the golden curlicued gates at the end of the palace gardens to the frozen fountain that dominates the middle of the square and on to the market that lies at the far end. On either side of the square, shops and businesses hem in the crowds—a florist, a bakery, a goldsmith. They're all closed to observe the spectacle.

Mother squeezes my hand for a moment. I think she's going to say something else, but she lets go, and I release a breath as she returns to Father, who stands staring steadily ahead, his bronze face unreadable.

Behind the gates, the towering arched oak doors of the palace open, their inlaid gold runes and patterns shining in the frozen sunlight. The parade begins. I should go now, take my chance, but I linger for a few seconds as the queen's Guard marches onto the steps, clad in black fur with gold sashes, swords glinting at their sides and crossbows braced to their backs. The royal family will follow.

I tear my gaze away and slip through gaps in the crowd back across the square until I'm in front of the ballet school, its turret rising above me almost as high as the palace itself.

Every business, school, and tavern is empty right now, as I knew they would be. Despite the fact that the music box is still missing and the peace treaty won't be signed without it, Queen Ana has declared today a public holiday. I silently thank her as I enter the narrow cobbled alley alongside the ballet school and run for the back door.

I'll have to be fast. I strip off my mittens and the cold surrounds my hands, chasing blood and warmth back into my body. I have seconds before my fingers become slow and clumsy. I pull a small, soft leather pouch from the folds of my skirts, then select two long, thin metal tools from the kit inside and insert them into the lock. My hands shake, and I glance behind me.

The crowd lets out another sigh of amazement. There are ten ice sculptures along the route the queen will walk, and they've just revealed the second. My heart beats fast, but I'm on schedule. The lock gives a satisfying *snick*, and I pull my mittens back on before I slip through the door. My hands are too important to risk.

Inside, I drop my kit to the floor and give it a little kick so it lands halfway under a rack holding countless pairs of satin ballet slippers. It pains me to lose it so, but it would only be taken away from me later. I hurry along the ground floor past changing rooms and through the pale wooden-floored studio that still smells of polish to the spiral stair-case at the back.

I stopped dancing a few months ago when I started my apprenticeship, but I know the school well. Sasha and I had lessons for years. When we were very little, I scuffed a brand-new pair of dance shoes in this studio and Sasha felt every part of my childish panic, knowing that our mother would be annoyed. She rubbed spit on the scuff for me, and when that didn't work, she risked borrowing our teacher's own resin to work out the marks while we hid behind a pile of furs on the coatracks.

That night I wasn't asleep when I should have been. But I pretended to be when our parents opened the bedroom door and a stripe of light fell over my bed. My mother said something I couldn't hear, and then my father said, "She loves her more than she loves herself." I never knew which one of us he was talking about, but it didn't matter then, and it doesn't matter now. I'm doing this for my sister because I know she'd do the same for me.

I climb the twisting iron steps quickly. On the first floor I fly down narrow corridors, then up small flights of stairs, up and up, until I reach the trapdoor to the turret.

The slats of wood are bound with black iron hinges, and a ring of black iron hangs down above my head. I grasp it and push. The door should swing open, but it doesn't. There's a weight against it. I push harder. Any second now they're going to unveil the third ice sculpture. The royal family will be at the palace gates, about to step out into the square. From the other end of the square, Lady Oleg-evna, steward of our closest neighboring province, Maga-danskya, will arrive, and the two leaders will meet in the middle—at the fountain built by Queen Ana's great-great-grandmother—to signify the peace between our nations. I should be up under the onion dome in the bell tower with my gear already assembled. There is no time.

Cheers go up from the crowd outside, their applause reaching me in a narrow, dusty corridor that smells of musty old costumes and stage makeup. My breath is coming too fast, and I fight to control it. I get underneath the trapdoor and throw my back at it, heaving as hard as I can. I'm starting to sweat. The wood gives with a sickly crack, warped by time and lack of use. I give thanks that I am tall and strong, and haul myself up into the frigid air of the bell tower.

I fasten the trapdoor behind me and peek over the edge onto the scene below. The square is filled with the queen's subjects, from beggar to lord. I've never seen such a sight before. I wish my parents weren't here.

The ice sculptures along the path glisten. Seven of the Guard march out in front of the family. Queen Ana walks slowly toward the fountain in middle of the square. Behind the queen is her husband, King Fillip, and their son, Prince Anatol, both in gray furs. Bringing up the rear, though it would have been her right to stand at her mother's side, is Princess Anastasia. She might even have been given the honor of carrying the music box.

If my sister hadn't stolen it.

The public part of the ceremony is going ahead as a sign of good faith, but my father says that the treaty won't be signed unless the box is found. Sasha told me many times that it's said to be the most beautiful thing in all the realm and worth so much it's practically priceless. She knew the history of it by heart too—how it belonged to Magadanskya but had long ago been stolen from them in battle and kept by us in Demidova since. None of the details would ever stick in my head—names and dates of queens and champions from long ago. Queen Ana returning the music box to its rightful owner after all these years was going to seal the peace treaty and save the country from war. Father says now she is nervous that the alliance will fail and the cold war will become an actual battle. Wars have been waged over less.

The royal family and their entourage pass behind the fourth sculpture—a giant pair of phoenixes with interlaced tail feathers, wings spread as if about to take flight—and it briefly distorts my view of them.

The queen is dressed in pure white, the diamonds and pearls on her *kokoshnik* shining like a halo around her head. Even at this distance, the elaborate black filigree around her eyes stands out. The royal *kosmetika* artist must have been up early this morning.

I turn away, place my back against the curved inside wall of the tower, and start pulling items from their secret hiding places. Two sections of metal from concealed compartments on either side of my boots. One thin section of wood from against the inner length of my calf.

I remove it all quickly, from every place—hat to necklace to soles of my boots—and assemble the parts into a whole. Every movement is precise, slick with three weeks of night-and-day practice. I wish my thoughts were as easy to click into place, but they're flying every which way.

The part with my clothes comes last. I won't be going back the way I came, and I can't run in skirts. I wrestle my way out of my coat and pull the yards of embroidered material away until my skirt and bodice are puddled on the floor. Underneath I have on my hunting gear, newly presented to me a month ago by my mother on the occasion of my and Sasha's thirteenth birthday—the official beginning of my apprenticeship to Mother and Sasha's to Father. Sasha got a set of Demidovan history books. I could barely convince her to put them down and share the birthday pastries with me.

I turn back to the parade in time to see the queen approach the fountain, which features a great stone mare galloping straight out of the ground and up into the air. Frozen plumes of water spray all around the animal as though it had burst into existence from some magnificent geyser hidden among the maintenance tunnels under the city.

I slide my fully assembled crossbow onto the ledge in front of me. Across the square, the clock tower strikes eleven. The sun is high over the domes of the palace, picking out the blue, gold, red, and stark white of their patterns. A light dusting of snow sits on the bulb of each dome like sugar icing on buns. The queen takes the hand of one of her guards and steps up onto the wide rim of the fountain. The giant back hooves of the stone horse and the jets of ice glint as she walks beside them.

The queen's family follows her onto the same wide stone brink Sasha and I used to play on until they are all raised above the people, facing a sector of the city. Prince Anatol is closest to me, the spot he stands in directly in line with my turret, as I knew it would be.

I try not to think about the time he offered me his hand when I fell from my horse. Still breathless, with a bruised leg and a crop of nettle stings, I had let him help me up. I let go of his hand as soon as I could. I'd been proud that my mother worked for his, that my family served his. It had felt strange to let him help me when he was a prince—like it should have been the other way around.

But some things are more important. I had to choose one of the royal family today, and my sister wouldn't want me to aim at the princess.

Lady Olegevna approaches on horseback, her deep-purple cloak sweeping the ground, her entourage on smaller mounts. They ride around the outer rim of the fountain, the crowd cheering, waving, clapping. This alliance has been hard won.

My finger hovers over the trigger of my crossbow as I take careful aim at Prince Anatol. I tried to teach Sasha to shoot on my target in our garden when we were ten. She did her best, but she didn't have the strength, and the bolt flew wide—straight through a pillowcase the housekeeper had hung on the washing line. Sasha's shocked face made me giggle, and we both ran away to the orchard, laughing fit to burst.

I'm not aiming at a practice target now. The prince's cloak is clasped at the throat with a golden fist, revealing the high-collared peacock-blue tunic he wears underneath. I've seen him in this apparel at a state function before—gold embroidery covers the front of it all the way up to the collar, which stands stiffly around his neck. As I steady my hands, lining him perfectly in my sights, he glances to his right and then yanks at his collar quickly before returning to waving at the crowd. If I wasn't where I am right now, that might make me smile. He's only a little older than I am, not yet fourteen.

The queen steps forward to address her subjects, and the crowd goes still and quiet. Little tremors pass all over my body. I tell myself they're because of the cold and take a deep breath. This is the hour that I've been waiting for. This is the minute that I've planned in secret for three weeks.

I shift the aim of my bolt a fraction to the left, just past Prince Anatol's shoulder, then I hold my breath, pray that he doesn't move, and shoot.

CHAPTER 2

The bolt sails through the air, whistling over the heads of the crowd. I peer above the ledge and watch it fly. My muscles tense. I can hardly bear to look, but I can't rip my gaze away either.

A couple of people in the crowd glance up, catching the movement above them, but the bolt flies true and lands with a *thunk* in the thick jet of ice behind the prince. I let out my breath in a relieved rush even as I'm lowering the crossbow to dismantle it.

For a few seconds, no one reacts. I gather up the pieces of my crossbow, tossing one to the floor and sliding another not back into the hidden compartment but just inside my boot instead. Then, as I pull my coat on and begin to tug my mittens onto my frozen hands, the prince spins to look behind him. Someone in the crowd points, and voices start rippling toward me.

I drop one of my mittens and snatch it up again. I want clues found, but it won't be a glove I leave in the trail. The queen pauses in her speech. Lady Olegevna's horse makes a soft noise, and the sound of its hooves on the cobbles carries above the rising voices as it moves skittishly.

The Guard bursts into life, and so do I, my chest tightening painfully. Half of the guardsmen draw their swords, the sound of metal on metal ringing out. I leap over the side of the turret and land on the tiled roof below. The other members of the Guard swing their crossbows into place, and I drop another section of my own weapon. It skitters over the tiles down into the gutter, and my heart goes straight over the edge with it as people start turning, looking, shouting, scattering.

I don't wait to see more. I run. I know that the rest of the Guard will pour from the palace and the royal family will be spirited away. I will be hunted.

The roof is crisp with frost on the shaded side. My boots slide, throwing me off balance. I catch myself, arms flailing in the air as I lose another piece of the crossbow. A little cry escapes me and I bite it off. Regulation Guard-issue boots thunder in the streets below. Orders are shouted that the queen's subjects are to clear the streets.

I launch myself onto the adjoining roof. On the adjacent side of the square, members of the Guard start scaling fire escapes. My breath comes out in steady streams of freezing mist as though I'm some kind of anti-dragon. I run.

Straight across the florist's roof, with the sun at its zenith in the sky.

At the far end of the florist's, there's a drop to the next roof. I expected it, but I pull up short. A loose fragment of tile clatters away and breaks as I reel on the edge. I look down at the shattered tile, then over to the Guard swarming through the streets and across the roofs toward me.

The ground is a long way down. But I can't have anyone questioning me about this later. If I'm to end up in Tyur'ma, my escape attempt has to look convincing.

I hold my breath, blood pulsing in my ears, and jump. I land hard on the cold tile. The shock shoots lightning fast through my bones and then I'm up, running, running to the next building and away down to the ground.

My hands fumble for the ladder propped against the side of the bakery—my route to the street. I don't feel it. My chest is heaving. I stretch farther around the gutter, moving my hands fast over the whole area. In desperation, I lie full-length on my stomach, bitter cold seeping through into my body, and reach as far as I can. It's gone. A panicked noise comes out of me before I can stop it.

A member of the Guard shouts behind me. I push to my feet. Another guard appears behind the first, and then I see the line of them, all following, all armed with swords, crossbows, or ceremonial daggers that are more than just decorative. My whole body tenses as I scan around me—the advancing guards, the drop to the cold, hard ground behind me.

I step forward and crouch into a full slide down the sloping roof of the bakery. It's only as I pick up speed, careering toward the edge, that I think what a horribly bad idea this was. How did I ever think I could pull this off?

A bolt flies past my neck, and as I fall off the edge of the building, a tiny section of my braid puffs into the air, each dark strand of hair falling around me as time slows down. The bolt falls with me, spinning end over end. A royal-issue bolt identical to the one now embedded in the ice of the fountain.

My body hits the awning, knocking the breath out of me. I bounce, roll, land on the street, and run. Bolts follow me across the empty square, some clattering on the cobbles, some hitting the deserted market stalls ahead of me. I flinch away from the whistling sounds and run headlong into the marketplace, upending a cart of potatoes, disappearing into the narrow, twisting pathways between the clutter of carts and stalls.

My legs burn, but I am silent as the hunter I could have been, and the guardsmen are loud with their heavy swords and boots. As I tear past a fruit cart, my sash snags on a nail, ripping the material. I grab the cloth and yank it free.

A hand shoots out from under the canvas draped around the cart and grabs my leg. I stifle a cry so it comes out as a rush of breath. "Under here," hisses a voice, and the hand beckons. I shake my foot, but the fingers cling to my boot. "Get under here. You can't outrun them." A dirty face pokes out, peering up at me around the curve of the cart wheel. It's a boy, dark-haired and pixie-faced. He's got bronze skin like mine, but even darker eyes than me. "You're going to lead them straight to me if you don't get under here," he says fiercely.

I don't know what else to do, so I fling the last remaining piece of my crossbow as far as I can, sending it soaring over the market. It must land on something soft—maybe the canvas cover of a stall—because it makes no sound. I duck under the draped material, and the boy yanks it back into place and puts a finger to his lips. He's crouched on the cobbles, bundled up in layers of fur that have seen better days. Next to him is a bulging bag, the long strap still crossed over his body.

Slowly, my heart stops pounding, and the boy brings his hand down, satisfied that we aren't going to be skewered at any second. "You're the one they're after?" he breathes. The words make soft clouds in front of his face. I nod. It makes little difference if he knows.

"What did you do?" He reaches for his bag and I shift back a little, but he puts out a hand and shakes his head. "It's okay. I was just getting this." He pulls out a packet of dates and slits it with a small knife I barely see before it's gone again. He holds the box out to me.

I don't move, or answer his question. This isn't part of the plan.

"Take one," he says. "You never know when you'll get the chance again."

I hadn't thought about it, but he's right, and I am hungry and thirsty. Sasha and I both love dates.

"Go on," he whispers, extending the box even farther. "I'm no poisoner."

I rip off my mitten and shovel a sticky fruit into my mouth, licking my fingers. "No, I don't suppose you are. Just a thief," I say, eyeing the bag.

"I prefer goods liberator, and you're no saint yourself if you're hiding here with me."

I have to smile, though it's strange to be in close quarters with such a boy. I don't think I've ever been face-to-face with a thief before; I've only heard about them.

"Who are you?" he asks, eating one of the dates himself.

I swallow.

"Well?" he demands.

I consider lying. "My name is . . . Valor," I say in the end. There's no point trying to protect my reputation or that of my family now. He'll find out soon enough what I've done.

The boy lets out a whisper-laugh. "Valor. After that, I should like to say that mine is Honesty," he says, "but you can call me Feliks. And so, Valor, how do you propose we get out of here?" He holds still to listen. The Guard is searching the market and spreading out into the streets that surround it. They will rip apart the whole city if they have to.

It's then that I realize I should never have hidden under here. I have to run farther or it will seem as though we're together. I work alone.

"You should stay right here," I say. Stay right here until I've led the Guard as far away as I can get them.

"What about you?" He says it like he's concerned, like we actually know each other and my fate matters to him. He's no older than I am—probably younger. A lump rises in my throat. I swallow it away.

"I have to go." I don't wait for him to answer. I whirl the canvas back, fling it into place behind me, and run, as far and as fast as I can, straight through the market. The streets are silent and deserted, everyone obeying the orders of the Guard. Everyone doing their part to help catch the would-be murderer of the beloved royal family.

I run past empty shops and find myself heading for the docks, for the open air and the cold sea. And for a moment, running down the road, I feel like I could keep going, keep running, silent in my boots. All the way to a ship that would leave the realm, taking me to a new world. My legs fly, bringing me closer to the district of warehouses. It's so quiet I can hear a dog bark miles away. I glance over my shoulder. Behind me, in the distance beyond the city, stretch the impossibly high walls of Tyur'ma. The prison fortress butts right up against the cliff face so the whole place seems hewn straight from the rock. Solid stone walls around the other three sides of the prison hide everything from sight. The only thing that could get over them is a bird. But I have seen birds shot out of the sky if they got too close.

Someone slams into me, sending me flying to the ground. My neck jerks to one side and I cry out. A blur of black and gold moves in front of me, but I'm up, light on my feet, dancing away from the sword she's drawn. Another guard appears behind me. He sheathes his sword and pulls his crossbow straight over his shoulder from his back. He aims right at my head as the first guard pushes forward, the tip of her sword at my heart.

"You . . . you have to arrest me." I can feel how thin the layer of skin and bone is between her blade and my beating heart. I never expected this. The queen can be a harsh judge, but she is fair; I thought she would want me alive.

The guard stares at me, and in her eyes I see the surprise at how young I am turn to cold determination. She's not going to arrest me—she's going to kill me right here in the street. My blood will spread on the snow and my mother and father will never know why. I try to speak again, but all I can do is shake my head.

Then she pulls a horn from her belt with her free hand, never taking her gaze off me, and blows a long note. I try not to flinch at the sound. I'm used to the hunting horn, but not when I am the prey. Guards start streaming in all around us. They converge in a group, and I'm surrounded. Right at that moment it starts snowing. Soft, fat flakes alight on the black *ushanka* the Guards wear.

I raise my face to the slow fall and the white wintry sky.

The guard with the sword starts speaking. "You are under arrest for the attempted murder of His Royal Highness Anatol of Demidova, crown prince of the Realm and brother of our future queen, Anastasia."

I almost sag to the ground with relief.

Two of the Guard position themselves on either side of me, two move in front, and the swordswoman and the guard with the crossbow cover the rear. They march me through the streets to the palace, the sword resting between my shoulder blades and the tip of the crossbow bolt pressing against the back of my neck.

As we approach the golden gates to the palace gardens, more of the Guard file from the palace itself. It makes me want to shout out that I'm not a killer, not dangerous, not what they think I am. But I can't let myself do that.

The golden gates open. I step into the royal gardens and take heart. I'm about to get exactly what I want.

CHAPTER 3

Snow begins to fall fast, sticking to my coat and to the frozen garden around us. Most of the Guard falls away, forming a line around the perimeter of the golden gates. I continue toward the palace steps with the six guards who surround me.

We pass one of the sculptures, unveiled what seems like days ago now. It's a huge replica of the *kokoshnik* that adorned Princess Anastasia's head during the ceremony. My sister would have loved it; she loves all delicate, beautiful things. The doors to the palace begin to open. The golden runes that inlay the ancient wood gleam as they catch the light. Sasha and I dreamed of entering the palace through these doors when we were very little. And as we grew older and were occasionally invited into the palace—always through one of the back entrances—we spent the nights after the visits hidden under her bedcovers making up stories about how we would walk through them one day.

None of the stories were quite like this, though.

My guards take me into a great hall with a mosaic-tiled floor and massive marble pillars stretching up to a mezzanine above. There is still no one around but my captors and me; it's as if the whole city has emptied. Our footsteps echo in the chamber. I swallow, already sweating in the warmth of the palace.

I catch sight of tall glass doors to my left, an explosion of exotic plants showing through. Green leaves and fronds and huge ruffled flowers of hot pink and incredible sun-bright orange. So it's true—the palace has a hothouse.

Then I am whisked along a corridor past heavy blue velvet drapes, yards of material that cascade from the high windows to the polished floors. And everywhere, there is gold.

Abruptly, the end of the corridor looms. One of the Guard pulls me to the right and down a spiral stone staircase. The temperature drops immediately as we descend into the earth under the palace.

The stone walls seem to breathe out the cold, stale air of the dungeon. My heart bangs loudly against the fine hunting gear I'm suddenly very aware of. Three dark cells open off a narrow corridor. Four more of the guards point their crossbows at me as the swordswoman orders me to stop and place my hands on the wall. She searches me roughly.

I think for a moment that she won't find the section of crossbow shoved into my boot, but she does.

I'm pushed into the middle cell. The iron door clangs behind me, the lock is turned, and the guards leave. I take in a shuddery breath and look at my cell. The back wall is solid stone, and the other three are iron bars. One torch burns in a sconce affixed to the wall of the corridor; it gives off only the dimmest light.

Something drips onto the floor behind me. I wrap my arms around myself.

"I'd move away from that side if I were you."

I spin to my right. A boy with a filthy face and an *ushanka* several sizes too large for his head nears the bars. He's thin but almost as tall as me, and his eyes are bright. It's the thief from the marketplace. Feliks.

"You got caught," I say, unaccountably disappointed. "What happened?" A weight hits the bars behind me, and something brushes one of my braids. I yelp, jumping forward.

Feliks shrugs. "Can't say I didn't warn you."

On the other side of the cell, a huge hand grasps the air where I was just standing. It's attached to a thick arm that has been pushed through the bars by its owner, whose face is in shadow like the rest of him.

The arm pulls back and disappears into the darkness. "He hasn't said one word yet," says Feliks.

"What does he want?" I ask in a whisper, sounding nowhere near as brave as I should.

Feliks lowers his voice conspiratorially. "I think he's hungry."

"What?"

"I'm joking. Probably. I've only been here for two minutes. They pulled me straight out from under that cart almost the second after you ran from it. How should I know what anyone else here wants?" He holds up his hands and smiles. One of his front teeth is smaller than the other, or maybe it's broken.

"It doesn't matter," I say. "I won't be here long."

Feliks frowns. "How do you know that?"

"Just . . . a feeling I have." I move into the corner closest to his side of the cell and sit on the floor, stretching out my legs. This is the dirtiest place I've ever seen, but every muscle in my body is tired.

"If it's okay with you, I won't put much store in that," he says. "Never trust a criminal." He sits down a little way from me, but his dirty furs brush mine as he does it. My arm stiffens, and he moves away again. Good. I'm not here to make friends. I can't have any distractions.

⁂

The torch outside the cell is burning low when Feliks stirs me out of my thoughts, nudging me in the ribs. "Someone's coming." He scoots away into the shadows at the back of his cell. It's the Guard. Just two of them this time. They unlock my cell and cuff my hands together. "Good luck," I hear a grim voice say as I'm marched up the stone steps and back into the palace.

I'm taken to the throne room. I recognize it from my father's descriptions. A few weeks ago he might have been present at the queen's side for an occasion such as this. The doors, white with polished gold lacework panels, swing open to admit me. At the end of a long room hung ceiling to floor with bright tapestries is a raised dais with four levels. The queen sits highest on a silver throne inset with pearls and backed by a huge fan of hundreds of peacock tail feathers. She wears her official robes of justice, deep blue with gold brocade on the cuffs and collar. Her eyes are still surrounded by the ceremonial black makeup, and she sits bolt upright, watching me as I walk down the length of the room. The closer I move, the louder my heartbeat gets.

On one side of the queen sits the king in his blue-and-gold tunic, and on the other, Princess Anastasia. Her throne is just a little lower than her father's, but in two months it will be raised above his to show that she has reached her thirteenth year. She has a blue-black kitten on her lap, and I fix my eyes on it as I'm brought before the royal family.

Prince Anatol is next to Anastasia, lower on his throne, and wearing the same blue and gold as his father. His hair is raven black, darker than that of the rest of his family. We've never been close—not like my sister and the princess—but still, I can't look at him either.

The queen raises and lowers her scepter, and I can't help but stare at the apple-size diamond at the head of it, topped by the royal emblem of a golden fist. "Just a girl," she says. "You may step back." It's clear she means the Guard, though she doesn't look at them.

And so I'm left standing there, alone, my hands cuffed in front of me, under the gaze of the queen of Demidova. I straighten and plant my feet shoulder width apart. She doesn't even seem to recognize me. Her own first hunts-woman's daughter, her own political adviser's eldest child—and she has no more idea of who I am than if I were a common thief in her dungeon.

"You are accused of attempting to murder His Royal Highness Prince Anatol. My son." Her voice snaps on the last two words.

I keep myself up straight. I can't afford to crumple now. I have to say what any reasonable person in my situation would say. "It wasn't me."

The queen raises an eyebrow. I can feel Prince Anatol's eyes on me. Sasha told me that when he's not riding, he's reading—often the same books my sister takes from the Great Library. Sometimes she would complain about how long he kept them in his chambers where she couldn't get them. He likes to work things out, to understand. And I don't want him to work out anything about why I'm doing this.

Queen Ana nods at someone behind me, and a guard carries forward a pile of items and lays it at her feet. There are the parts of my crossbow, my skirts, the pouch of tools I used to pick the lock of the ballet school, and the bolt pulled from the ice of the fountain. On top of these things, he lays a torn scrap of material.

"What is that?" asks Princess Anastasia.

The queen doesn't answer; she just regards my sash until her daughter follows her gaze to the tear in it.

"Do you still deny it was you?"

"Yes, Your Highness."

"Who are you working for?"

"I work for no one." It's the first bit of truth from my mouth, and somehow, Prince Anatol can tell. His head tilts when I say it.

"And yet the weapon you used, part of which was found on your person, is of royal issue. Do you care to explain that, Valor Raisayevna?"

So she *does* know who I am. Knows, and doesn't care.

"Is this retribution?"

"Your Highness?"

The queen's jaw tenses. "Is this your idea of paying us back for the disgrace and banishment of your parents? It is your sister you have to thank for that, Valor, not me."

My heart squeezes, but I say nothing.

It's then that a voice sounds outside the throne room. Even muffled by the distance and the thick walls I recognize it. My mother. I can't make out the words, only the tone. Beseeching. Desperate. I almost cry her name, almost run to her.

There's a single bang at the door. My pulse races, my body leaning almost against my will toward my mother. I want that door to open. I long for it to. But it doesn't.

The queen's gaze had snapped up at the sound, but now it falls back to me. "Or perhaps your family intended to *further* disrupt the peace treaty that I have worked *years* for." Her tone is cold, furious. "Do you know how close we are to war? Did your parents plan this? Did your mother give you that weapon?"

Anastasia touches the queen's arm with a gloved hand. "Mother, surely they wouldn't send their only remaining child to do this, knowing the consequences. Not after Sasha."

I picture my mother on the other side of the wall in the throne room, being dragged away, made to leave the palace. But the princess saying my sister's name has given me strength and purpose. I hold myself up straight. "No. My parents know nothing of this. They had no idea."

The queen nods. Her shoulders drop a little, as if she is saddened. "I will have word sent to them of what you have done. And where you have gone."

My stomach clenches. This is it. I focus on the image of my sister's face, not thinking about Mother and Father. They will understand, eventually. I think about Sasha standing here—perhaps in this very spot—three weeks ago, after she was arrested for stealing the music box from the palace. Returning the box to Lady Olegevna was to be the pinnacle of this day—a treasure finally delivered to its rightful owners.

Did Sasha look at Princess Anastasia as her mother handed down her sentence? She was apprenticed to Father as I was to Mother. In time she would have become the princess's adviser, just as my father advised her mother.

Queen Ana stands to deliver my sentence. I know what she's going to say. I know it, and I want it. And yet I can't stop the shiver that goes from my scalp to the soles of my feet.

"For the crime of attempted murder of a member of the royal family in the realm of Demidova, I sentence you to life in prison, beginning in Tyur'ma."

CHAPTER 4

The queen remains standing as she orders the Guard to take me away, but I don't know how I manage to do the same. Everything inside me pulls in opposite directions. I've tried so hard to make my plan perfect, and it worked. It actually worked. But Queen Ana's words—a life sentence—it's like being hit by one of my crossbow bolts.

I'm marched back to my cell on legs that feel like they aren't mine, not seeing the gold, not feeling the spicy warmth of the palace. Cold stone steps. Cold, stale air. I'm thrown back into my cell and have just enough presence of mind to move to the side closest to Feliks's cell. Iron clangs, and it's quiet and dark again.

"Where did they take you?" Feliks's grubby face presses up against the bars. I shuffle over to the back of the cell to the straw meant to serve as bedding. It's doing a better job of being mouse food.

"To the throne room." I sit down, even though the floor is damp and the stone walls are rough.

His thin fingers wrap around the bars. "Before the queen?"

"Before the whole royal family."

His eyes go wide. The dirt on his forehead creases. "You're no thief. What did you do?"

I rub my hands up and down my arms. I'm used to the cold, but I can't seem to stop shivering. "I shot a crossbow at Prince Anatol," I say. I can hardly believe I did it, now that it's all over. "Didn't you see it?"

He shakes his head. "While all the fancy folk were conducting their business, I was conducting my own. You *killed* the prince?"

The hulking shadow in the other cell grunts and shifts. The boy lowers his voice. "*Why?*" He moves away from me, just a little bit, but I see it, and I feel it too; it cuts me inside. He's shocked. A dirty-faced urchin who's been arrested and thrown in the palace dungeon is shocked. By me. By what I've done. I knew this would happen; the royal family are loved.

I didn't expect it to make me so sad.

"I didn't kill anybody. I didn't hit him," I say. "Didn't even mean to hit him." Anatol's always been a little serious, never smiling and ready to laugh like his sister, but neither has he ever sulked the way she could sometimes. And he's as good a rider as I am, if not quite as skilled a marksman with his bow. I would never hurt him.

The torch on the wall burns brightly. They must have replaced it when they brought me back. Feliks moves closer again, cautiously. Black flakes of iron crumble from the bars under his fingers. "Why did you do it, then? Is everything all right up there?" He reaches through the bars and taps the side of my head with a grimy fingernail, then quickly pulls his arm back.

"Yes, everything's fine up there, thank you very much." I turn to him, and he's grinning now, front teeth big and white in the torchlight. There's something about him I can't help but like. I feel like the old me when I talk to him, not the new me who keeps everything secret and plans and plots for weeks on end.

"I needed to do something bad enough to get myself in here, and I'm a good shot, so it seemed like the obvious choice. I don't have anything against Prince Anatol." I think about him staring at me in the throne room. I might not have anything against him, but he's got something against me now.

"Now I *know* there's something wrong with you. You want to live in the dungeon? You haven't seen the food they bring yet."

I shake my head. "Not the dungeon. Tyur'ma."

His mouth and eyes go perfectly round in his face. "But *why*?"

I glance across to the other cell, but there's no movement. The shadows are black and blacker. I lower my voice anyway. "Do you remember a few weeks ago, when the music box was stolen from the palace?"

He snorts. "Remember? It's all anybody talked about. Wait a minute—that was *you*?"

I grip the bars between us, pulling myself right up close to him. Wisps of dark hair poke out from under his *ushanka*. "No. It was my sister, Sasha." Saying her name out loud makes my throat hurt. I swallow. "They sent her to Tyur'ma. She wouldn't confess where the music box was, and—"

The boy watches me. "And now the queen can't give it back to Lady what's-her-name?" he says.

"Exactly."

"So now she's in prison, and you're going there too."

I nod.

"Did she get a life sentence?" he asks.

"Yes."

He swallows. "Did you?"

I nod again and try to rip down the creeping vine of fear that I don't know what I'm doing, that there was some other way to help Sasha. Something else I could have done.

He huddles into himself and rests against the wall. I think he isn't going to say anything else. The drip in my cell hits the floor with a wet echo.

"You must love her a lot to give up your whole life just to be with her." He sounds sad and thoughtful.

"We're sisters," I say. "Twins. I don't *have* a whole life without her."

Sasha had a clockwork prince once. She loved it so much. She took it apart to see how it worked, and cried bitterly when she couldn't make it whole again. It took me three days to put it back together. But I didn't stop then, and I won't stop now.

I'm not doing all this just to *be* with Sasha, though. At least not in Tyur'ma. I have much more in mind than that. But I'm not telling Feliks about my plans.

"Where is your family?" I ask him.

"Got none." His voice is small now. "But it's nice to meet someone who loves the one they have so much, Valor."

"It's nice to meet you too, Feliks," I say. And I mean it.

I'm jolted awake by the clank of my door unlocking. The gloomy corridor outside the cells is filled with dark shapes that block the torchlight. I spring to my feet and back up against the wall, heart pounding. Suddenly four more torches blaze to life, and I see guards fitting the torches to sconces all along the dank wall in front of my cell.

Feliks is beside me. I wait for the guards to do something, but they only file out of the corridor and back up the stone steps. Feliks and I look at each other, confused. Then I see his face change, all the color slipping out of it. He backs away, and I spin to see a huge figure inside my cell.

His arms are banded with muscle so thick that it pushes them away from his body. They're bare of the uniform the Guard wear, covered instead from shoulders that look like enormous glazed hams to thick fingers with black-inked tattoos—crisscrossed latticed patterns, great eyes, and wild animals with bared teeth.

I stumble back again until I hit the cold stone wall. He steps forward so he's towering over me. I'm not short for a girl my age, but my eyes are level with the middle of his chest. I look up and take in a sharp breath. Staring down at me is the red-eyed face of a sneering demon, its horns twisting up over the man's chin and ending at either corner of his mouth.

Only Peacekeepers, the prison guards at Tyur'ma, have these marks. The more they have, the longer they've worked there. And this one has tattoos snaking down under the collar of his black garb. He's come to collect me for transportation.

I remember, with a sudden rush, sitting in the dark at the top of the wooden stairs in our house five or six years ago, listening to my parents and Mother's hunting party talk about the prison and its Peacekeepers. They'd caught a girl out poaching on the queen's lands. My mother, as head huntswoman, had no choice but to bring her before the queen, who had in turn sentenced her.

The prison had been set up to keep child prisoners separate from the adults, who worked harder and longer hours in the mines deeper in the mountains. But my father wasn't happy with the conditions there. Queen Ana's stance on crime was popular with the people, but Father said heavy punishments made no difference. He wanted to overhaul the system and use education and greater numbers of apprenticeships instead. The adults discussed it for some time. It wasn't until I was stiff and cold and falling asleep that I heard a sniffle in the dark, back by Sasha's bedroom. I slipped away before my mother could hear, reaching for my sister and finding her curled against her door frame, sobbing.

I pulled her into her bedroom, where she shivered and clung to me. "What are you doing out of bed listening to that?" I whispered at her, worried that I'd be the one to take the blame. We were twins, but I was born first. She'd always been more sensitive than me, never suited to follow our mother into the hunt.

She rubbed her eyes and let me lead her to the bed. I pulled back the heavy quilts and got in with her. "You were listening," she said. "I wanted to hear too. Why did Mama take that girl to that place? It sounds horrible."

I shushed her, stroking the dark hair, wet with tears, at her temple. "The girl was a thief. She stole from the queen's lands. Mother had no choice."

"But, Valor." Sasha looked up at me with big dark eyes, shining in the starlight. "What the hunters said about the

Peacekeepers. Do they really chain the children and make them work? Do they really . . . do they kill them if they run away?"

"And what if they do?" I said. "It's their job, just as it's Mother's to hunt the deer and the boar for royal banquets and keep the city and the villages safe from the mountain cats and beasts."

She burrowed her head into my neck.

"Peacekeepers are just people, and you and I will never have to meet one anyway, so go to sleep and forget about it."

Her chest was still hitching, but she nodded, her hair tickling my chin.

As I stand now in front of someone I told my sister we would never meet, I can't stop thinking of her. How terrified she must have been.

I try to get myself under control. *They're just tattoos*, I tell myself, but I still squeak when he reaches out and takes hold of me. He's carrying a dark mass of metal. His huge, inked hands cover mine, and something cold and heavy drags my arms down.

Feliks sucks in a breath, and I hear him scuttle across his cell to a corner. The Peacekeeper's gaze darts up and latches on to the movement as if he can see in the dark. He moves out of my cell, dragging me with him like I'm a cabbage leaf, and unlocks Feliks's cell too.

"I'm not going to Tyur'ma," says Feliks. "It was just food I took. But I'll go back to being an apprentice and never steal anything again. I'll go back, I swear. Valor, if we go into that place, we don't come out again. I don't think—"

The Peacekeeper steps toward Feliks, shockingly fast for such a big man, and Feliks rushes forward, the whites of his eyes showing as he twists his head toward the stone steps. He's going to try to escape. And I know what Peacekeepers do to children who try to escape.

I lurch forward and snag Feliks with the chains between my wrists, holding on to him for everything I'm worth while he twists and bucks his thin body. It takes every bit of strength I have to stay on my feet. I can feel my shoulder bruising in the Peacekeeper's grip.

"What are you doing?" Feliks hisses at me. Straw slips under my boots, but I don't let go.

"We're ready to go," I say to the Peacekeeper. Not that he needs my approval or permission. He stares at me, still completely impassive. I didn't expect him to be silent. But what is there to say, after all? We're going with him whether we like it or not, and if Feliks gets out of my grasp and tries to run, he'll be dead.

The Peacekeeper lets go of me suddenly, spins around, and clamps irons onto Feliks's wrists, holding both of us by lengths of chain. Feliks wrenches himself away from me and says in a furious whisper, "I could have made it. Now

I'm stuck, and it's all your fault." He's breathing hard, his clothes bunched around him.

I don't know what to say. He couldn't have made it. I don't think he could have, anyway. The Peacekeeper moves too fast; he's too strong. Feliks would be lying in the straw now, and I'd be leaving the palace dungeon alone.

He's right, though—if he had any chance, it's gone, and it's my fault. I don't know why I grabbed him. I'm doing this for Sasha. I had it all planned, and I told myself a thousand times to stick to the plan.

I stare at Feliks, who just stands there now, looking sullen. We're both wearing thick iron cuffs around our wrists. There's a longer chain between us that links us together, and yet another chain that connects to a spiked belt around the Peacekeeper's middle. I have no idea how he moved so fluidly, so fast. The chains ripple out between us, heavy and cold.

"You will call me Peacekeeper Rurik," he says, and he walks forward swiftly, dragging both of us along behind him while the depth of his voice reverberates in my head.

Feliks scowls at me as we're led up the stone steps. The Guards who lit the torches before are waiting. They surround us as we march so we see nothing of the palace, only feeling its warmth until the great doors open again before us.

We stand on the threshold, looking out on the deserted square. Outside it's dark, and it surprises me at first, but of course it's nighttime. Of course hours have been passing for everyone else while my whole life changed. I can never change it back now.

I'm standing on the palace steps thinking about that, chained and surrounded by the Guards, when, through the gaps between the black uniforms around me, I catch a flash of blue and gold. Prince Anatol stands in front of the glass doors of the hothouse, staring at me.

I try to steel myself against his stare, tell myself that soon I'll be with Sasha, but heat floods my face anyway. Something about the way he looks at me makes me suddenly glad that we're leaving the palace. Soon I'll be at Tyur'ma, away from Anatol's cold, curious eyes.

The Guards move forward as one, Peacekeeper Rurik with them, and Feliks and I are jerked out into the biting cold to Tyur'ma, where I'll be spending the next three years of my life, if I live that long. Or so they think.

CHAPTER 5

The night is clear, thousands of stars studding the deep purple sky. My breath spreads in icy clouds in the frigid air. At the end of the palace garden, a guard opens the golden gates, and it's only Peacekeeper Rurik, Feliks, and I who step through into the deserted cobblestone square, our boots silent on the fresh snow.

I wonder if the order to stay inside has been extended until I've been taken away. I don't think I could bear to see my parents' faces anyway. It's better that I extinguish the little girl inside me who wants them to come and take me home. I glance across at Feliks, but he stares straight ahead, his cuffed wrists out in front of him. Our chains make a soft clanking where they meet each other at the back of Peacekeeper Rurik's belt.

We go through the empty market, stalls now covered

in heavy sacking, into quiet, dimly lit streets, out past the business district and into narrow streets lined with homes, until we reach the city limits.

Roads lead off in several directions to other towns, cities, and villages, but straight ahead lies the road to Tyur'ma—and in the distance, the prison itself, fiercely lit by a thousand torches, as it is every night. There is no darkness around Tyur'ma. No shadow to hide in.

"Halt." Peacekeeper Rurik reaches around and takes a chain in each hand. He leads us to a solid wooden cart pulled by a pair of monstrous black horses wearing blinders. They snort and stamp, their coats inky black against the snow.

On the back of the cart is an iron-barred cage. Peacekeeper Rurik pulls us in like fish on a line. I have to try hard not to pull away. I don't want to be close to him again.

He runs the chains through the loops on his belt, shoving us through the door and tethering us to either side of the cage. Feliks watches everything he does, taking in the locks and the keys, which are hanging from the thick, spiked belt around Peacekeeper Rurik's waist.

I shake my head at him, in case he's thinking of trying something else, though I desperately want a good look at those keys myself.

"Leave me alone," Feliks whispers. "Haven't you done enough?" He stares at me defiantly as the cart lurches forward and out onto the road.

"Prisoners speak only when spoken to," says Peace-keeper Rurik. His massive frame fills the seat on the front of the cart, the reins grasped in his hands looking like the delicate hair ribbons Sasha used to wear before she began her position at the palace. After that Princess Anastasia insisted Sasha use her own personal hairdresser. It was really more favor than she should have shown, which is why I try not to think about Sasha betraying that trust and stealing the music box. I still don't know why she did it.

Instead, I think of Sasha running through the house shrieking as I chased her with an arctic fox pelt over my head. Or Sasha reading Father's books by the fire in his office while he discussed matters of state that put me to sleep, but which Sasha would listen to all night if she could manage to keep still for long enough that Father would forget she was there.

Are you crying? Feliks mouths to me. He's trying to sneer, but he looks like he could cry too, which makes my eyes blur even more.

I shake my head and press a finger to my lips. Tyur'ma is run on rules. Rules that must not, *cannot* be broken. We both have to get used to that now.

The city disappears behind us not long after we enter the forest, snow blanketing all noise apart from the creak and groan of the cart and the snorting of the horses. The mass of light that is Tyur'ma gets closer as we leave the forest and reach the plains. The queen's lands run for miles and miles around the prison, vast expanses where herds of goats and sheep roam. Where anyone who made it past the towering stone walls of Tyur'ma would be seen before they could find anywhere to hide.

An icy breeze blows, catching the topmost layer of snow and carrying icy crystals across my face. I shiver. A howl from across the plains snaps my eyes wide open. I glance to Peacekeeper Rurik. One of his hands rests on a crossbow by his side.

An answering howl bounces back, and suddenly a whole pack is calling out as another challenges it. I scan the plains but there's nothing in sight, only starred black sky and iced white ground. Then, in the distance, I see a silhouette against the snow. The wolf stands almost as tall as one of the horses pulling our cart. I try to force down the panic I feel, chained and defenseless in the cart. If my mother were here, I'd feel safe. Now I have to rely on Peacekeeper Rurik.

He murmurs to the horses and we jolt forward, faster and faster toward Tyur'ma. My arms, held up by the chains, become stiff, and then Feliks kicks me with his boot. We have arrived.

The white mountains tower in front of us, cold and ancient, glittering with snow and cruel, jagged rock. These are the borders of Demidova. On the other side of the mountains to the east lie Lady Olegevna's lands, Magadanskya. To the west lies Pyots'k. Their queen has been petitioning Queen Ana to let her use the Demidovan ports for months. Queen Ana has refused offers of gold, knowing that the queen of Pyots'k wants to use the ports to launch warships, not trade ships. Part of the function of the alliance with Magadanskya is to strengthen Demidova against the requests, which my father says have become increasingly demanding of late.

I take one last look at the wolves, judge the distance between them and us, and turn to Tyur'ma.

A path twists up the mountain, leading to the gates of the fortress. The black walls tower up into the sky farther than any that I have ever seen. Block after enormous block of stone reaches away from the ground until it seems impossible that it was built by anyone but a giant. Set into the wall is a portcullis, gridded in iron, that looks hardly big enough for us to pass through.

The horses labor up the path, their hooves scrabbling on the loose stones that litter the way. A grinding, as of cogs and chains, starts, and the portcullis rattles slowly up. I pull my hands away from the bars just in time to stop my fingers scraping on stone as we pass through. The doorway is a hair's breadth wider than the cart.

Inside, another wall stretches away, forming a narrow passageway all around the perimeter. Feliks takes in a breath at the sight of the double wall. We exchange a look as Peacekeeper Rurik halts the horses and opens our cage.

The chains rattle as Peacekeeper Rurik unfastens them from the bars and links them back to his belt. We leave the cart behind and walk along the stone passageway between the two walls. Above us the thin strip of sky is now deepest black. Our way is lit by torches, burning brightly at intervals on the inner wall. Then we turn a corner and there's a solid iron door, no bigger than any door in the most humble of homes. It opens inward, and we step through into another iron cage that surrounds the door.

I am inside Tyur'ma. Adrenaline buzzes through me, waking up my tired limbs and jolting thoughts of Sasha back into my head.

Flat, snow-covered ground stretches away, hemmed in on three sides by the great walls and at the back by a wickedly sharp white cliff rising up into the clouds.

Twisted, wind-whipped icicles hang from the gutters and ledges of every watchtower and cellblock. And walking toward us, with a pleasant smile on her face, is a woman dressed in the pale gray furs of the queen's court. I recognize them—they're exactly the same as those my parents wore until this past month—and suddenly I miss Mother and Father so much my whole chest feels like it might burst. I saw those gray furs every day of my life. My parents were proud to wear them, proud that one day Sasha and I would too. Mother hasn't been the same since she lost the right and had to put hers away.

Maybe they're imploring friends to petition the queen at this very moment. Maybe they're too sad, too broken to do anything. Maybe they've become angry with me.

The woman draws close to us and nods at Peacekeeper Rurik, who pushes me and Feliks through the cage and out into the open. When she looks at me, I feel my face flush, even though I'm half-frozen. Her mouth might be smiling, but her eyes are not. They're a steely blue, and she looks at me as though she's reaching into my head, like she can see every part of my plan. Like she knows why I'm here. I shiver.

"I am Warden Kirov, the head of Tyur'ma. You will address me as Warden." She turns and starts walking briskly back toward the buildings. Peacekeeper Rurik follows, and so do we, still cuffed and chained to his belt.

"You will work in the mines, or anywhere else in the prison we tell you to. You will eat when you are told to, you will sleep when you are told to, you will work when you are told to. If you reach the age of sixteen while you are here, you will be transferred to the adult prisons in the mountains. If you are caught with contraband items, you will be punished. If you cause trouble with any other inmates, you will be punished."

She delivers this speech almost as if she has timed it to last exactly until we reach a stone building with a single iron door punched into its side. Then she opens the door and nods to Peacekeeper Rurik, who starts unchaining me, but not Feliks.

"In Tyur'ma's three-hundred-year history, no one has ever escaped. If *you* try to escape, you will be punished. Unless you are killed," she says, still wearing the same pleasant smile.

Feliks looks up at me, his face a mix of anger and fear and reproach as we're separated and our cuffs are removed. Then he is pulled away toward another building, looking tiny at Peacekeeper Rurik's side.

"Come now, Valor Raisayevna," says the warden. I tear my gaze from Feliks at the sound of my name. Of course she knows who I am. And why I've been sent here.

"Revenge is something you'll find little use for here," she says, and she steps forward into the building. She thinks I tried to kill Prince Anatol as vengeance for the queen sending Sasha here. Which is exactly what I wanted. It still burns me with shame to think about it, though, so I try not to. I'm so close now, so close to where Sasha is. I can't let a little thing like pride get in my way.

I follow the warden onto a stone balcony just inside the door and hold back a gasp. In front of me is a vast, hollowed-out cavern with walls and floor of stone. There are four levels—one below me and two above—all connected by tiny flights of stone steps cut into the walls. And at every level there are cells, recessed into the stone, with black iron bars.

I try not to breathe too fast, but my heart is skipping and sinking all at the same time at what I've done. This is the most notorious prison in Demidova. Behind the bars in each of these cells is every criminal under the age of sixteen from the entire realm.

But my sister, Sasha, is here. Somewhere, she is here.

And I'm going to break her out.

I crane my neck to see the other inmates, but all the cells are darkened. It's still some time before dawn, I think, and the prison is silent.

Crushed snow falls from my boots and makes a slushy puddle at my feet. Warden Kirov extends her arm as if offering me the choice of heading up the stone steps to my left. "Your cell is this way."

I wind my way up the steps, hugging the wall. And that's when I realize there are no rails, no bars, nothing to stop me from falling off the steps and down to the stone floor below. It's the same on every level and on the pathways outside the cells.

"We find there's a lot more compliance when everyone is focused on not falling to their deaths," says the warden pleasantly.

I look down. The steps are worn in the middle, some of them chipped and uneven. They're barely wide enough for my boots. As we walk, the darkened lower level twists farther away until I emerge onto a narrow ledge. The cells stretch out in front of me. I try not to stare, but I can't stop myself from snatching glances as we walk past. Sasha could be in any of them. Even the one I'm heading for.

I take a deep breath and try to stop the nerves fluttering in my stomach. All I can see are iron bunks bolted to the walls and dark shapes lying in each of them.

"Stop here," says the warden. She unlocks a cell and pulls the narrow door open. "In you go, then, Valor." I hesitate, looking at the shadowy lump in the lower bunk and realizing with disappointment that, of course, it isn't Sasha. I can't see her face, but this girl is bigger. I squeeze my hands into fists inside my mittens and swallow hard. I have to go in there. This is why I came. There's no point making a fuss now—not that it would do any good.

I take a little step, then another, until I'm on the other side, inside the cell. The warden swings the door shut and locks it. Suddenly the shadows and the cold and the stone walls are all around me.

"We'll be watching you with great . . . interest," says the warden, and then she turns and walks away. I'm left in silence. Who did she mean by "we"? I don't have time to think about it for more than a second. The girl in the bunk, who had been facing the wall as if she were asleep, moves.

I push my hair back from my face and dig out a nice smile. "I'm Valor," I begin.

"Shut up," says my cellmate.

CHAPTER 6

My new cellmate turns over quietly on her thin mattress. I can't tell what she looks like in the dim torchlight—only that she's taller than me. I would step away, but I can already feel the cold of the stone wall at my back. The bars cast darker shadows across her body, striping the gray with black.

"Pardon?" I say.

"Well, if you aren't going to shut up, at least lower your voice," says the shadow peevishly. "We're not supposed to talk, and I don't want to earn an infraction. You'll wake up Daria in the next cell, and she'll inform on us."

"Inform," I repeat, more to myself than her. I'm still just standing there in front of her, but I'm not sure what else to do.

"Don't you know how it works here?" she asks, impatient now.

"No, I don't. I must have overlooked that page in the handbook," I say. This is not going the way I had envisioned it at all. "Look," I say. "My name is Valor—"

"Good for you. Now shut up."

I know I should stop, but I'm so close now. "I just want to find my sister. She's here too, and I would . . . I'd like to find her."

"Last piece of advice: you should be in your bunk," says the girl. "We're supposed to be in them until we're told to get up."

Clearly she's not going to listen to me unless I'm following the rules, so I step forward, reaching for the top bunk.

"*Not* until you wash those hands," she hisses.

I stop with my hands still out. "What?"

"Over there. There's water over there."

In the murky shadows at the back of the cell, I can just make out a basin on the floor.

"Quick," she says impatiently.

I briefly think about kicking the basin at her head. "Is this a rule?" I ask, trying to remember everything the warden said.

The shadow snorts softly. "*This* is just good sense."

I hesitate, but then pull my mittens off and shuffle into the dark, bending to the basin. The water feels like frozen needles on my fingers, and I can't stop a little gasp when it reaches my wrists.

"Give them a good scrub. You're probably *covered*."

I can't help but be a little indignant. "Covered in what, exactly? I assure you, my hands are clean. And if they weren't before, they are now."

"It's not the dirt you can *see* I'm worried about." The shadow sniffs and turns back to the wall.

Wonderful.

She didn't even react when I said my sister was in here. I wish I had a silver tongue like my father and my sister do. Sasha could convince anyone of anything, even the queen. Not long before Anastasia's ninth birthday, the princess enlisted Sasha's help in order to get yet another pet. She'd been begging Queen Ana for a hairless cat, to no avail. But once Anastasia told Sasha about it, my sister set her mind to making it happen. Documents about the benefits of hairless cats were prepared—including a statement from the royal doctor about the lack of hair on the animal being much more suited to Anastasia's governess at the time, who sneezed alarmingly around Anastasia's other pets. There was even a contract, signed by the princess, stating she'd be solely responsible for care of the creature.

The queen was charmed. The hairless kitten was purchased.

If Sasha were here, her words would be a dazzling ice sculpture, beautiful and blinding. Mine are a blunt wooden training sword thwacking away at the inert lump that is my cellmate.

I stand up, my cold, wet hands dripping water onto the floor. All day I've been pulled tight as the drawing mechanism on my crossbow. I've been chased through the streets and threatened and dragged across the city and terrified half to death for hours. Nothing has ever looked as inviting as the bed in front of me. Even the sight of the dirty material stretched over rough straw until some of the seams have burst doesn't put me off.

I reach for the iron bars of the bunk to pull myself up. From deep underneath the ground, a rumbling starts. My muscles tense, and I brace myself. The noise grows louder, as if the earth is going to split. Suddenly, light streams into the cell, as though a thousand torches have been lit. I take a shaky breath. My cellmate leaps out of her bunk and stands rigid in front of the cell door. She *is* taller than me, by at least two inches.

"What—?"

"Shh," she spits. Her hair is lighter than mine, the color of sand. Her eyes and skin are too. I've never seen eyes so light. She might be from Pyots'k. And I must look terrified, because she relents. Over the grinding, rumbling noise coming from beneath and above us she shouts, "*That* is us being told to get up. And if you know what's good for you, you will stand up straight and close that endlessly flapping mouth of yours." She swings back around, her braids swinging with her, and I bite off my retort. My mouth is no such thing.

A chill breeze blows cold but fresh air into the cell, and the light becomes bright as day, making me blink. The walls are rough, as is the stone of the ceiling. Apart from the iron bunks bolted to the wall and the basin, the cell is bare. The floor is of the same stone, but worn smooth with time and use. My eyes feel gritty. I look to the bunk longingly.

The grinding noise stops and silence rings in my ears for a second before another noise begins, a sort of metal-on-metal screeching filling the whole cavern of the cell-block. I want to cover my ears, but that might be against the rules too. The cell door, which had swung open to admit me such a short time ago, starts sliding into the stone wall as if being rolled back.

When the noise finally stops and our cell is an open-mouthed cave, my cellmate's stance changes. She braces herself as though she's about to hurl a javelin. Instead, she hurls herself out into a sudden torrent of girls pouring past on the pathway, a human river of tightly packed furs and faces, all of them strangely silent.

I stand frozen, unsure what to do other than watch. Any one of them could be Sasha. I search every face that passes, but I'm sure I miss some, and Sasha isn't as tall as I am anyway. We might be twins, but she's slighter, with delicate hands meant for turning the pages of a book, not drawing a bow or a knife.

I watch until the rush begins to ebb, then I peep out of the cell. My face almost hits the spiked belt of a Peacekeeper. Above me, his face is inked into a black-and-white chessboard. I'm already tired and twitchy, and he makes me jump, which is undignified at best.

"You are not outside your cell at the designated time," he says. His voice is flat and emotionless, almost bored.

I clear my throat and summon up my voice. "I'm sorry, but I didn't know—"

"First infraction." The Peacekeeper pushes his ink-checkered hand into a leather pouch at his waist and steps forward.

I stumble back, forgetting whatever it was I would have said, and bump into the wall outside my cell. His hand moves up, and I don't know whether to yell or run or fight whatever he's going to do. I end up holding my breath, so I don't squeak while he tilts my head with one massive hand and smears something gritty in a line down my forehead. My mind races around trying to work out what he's done, what it means.

I register that I can see the sky with my head tilted up— it's an early morning pink-white—but it just confuses me. It's not until the Peacekeeper steps away and says "Move" that I realize the rumbling noise was the roof of the cellblock rolling away, just as the cell doors did. The cavern is exposed to the chilly air. I've never seen anything like it. Down below, on ground level, the last of the prisoners file through the door out to the grounds.

"Move," says the Peacekeeper again, reaching back into his pouch. I don't need to be told twice. I take off like a winter hare, running along the ledge outside the cells as fast as I dare, then down the worn steps cut into the wall, reaching the door just before it shuts with a metallic clang. Behind the cellblock the white mountains rise, jagged as leopard's teeth. The stone fortress rears up out of a mountainside, cutting into the arctic sky above it all.

The girl at the back of the line is small, almost running to keep pace with the others. I catch up to her, cold stinging my cheeks and running like ice water into my throat and lungs, but I pause as soon as I reach her. We're heading for a building I didn't see earlier, one that was camouflaged in the snow. One made entirely of ice. It glows an eerie blue in the morning light.

I remember myself and run forward. Snow crunches under my boots as I hurry along, dodging out of the line so I can see ahead. It does me no good; all I can see are dark braids and brown furs, and none of them are Sasha.

I should never have encouraged her obsession with the music box. Two weeks before it disappeared, we were eating dinner before the fire in the kitchen. Mother and Father were working and the housekeeper was busying herself elsewhere, so we were alone and indulging in our favorite topic of conversation—the Royal Parade.

"We'll have to watch from the square, of course, but Father will be able to find out exactly where we should stand for the best view," I said, picking up chicken with my fingers. Sasha saw me and put her fork down to do the same.

Her eyes were bright in the firelight as she shook her head. "I know exactly where it is in the palace, and yet not one glimpse, no matter how many times I engineer a reason to be in the same room." She sighed, using her now shiny fingers to eat mashed potatoes.

She was fascinated by mechanisms and clockwork. Combined with her interest in Father's work and all the old stories in her history books, the level of her excitement was no surprise. Sasha had made it her mission to see the music box up close before the parade, and everyone knew it. When I think about her stealing it, I wonder whether she ever meant to, or whether she just wanted to look at it, to admire it for a while. I should have realized.

"Ow!"

"Oh, saints, I'm sorry," I cry. The girl in front of me is facedown on the ground. She comes up spitting snow. In my haste I've plowed right over her. I crouch to offer my hand, and from nowhere she shoots out her foot and hooks the back of my knees. My legs buckle, and I fall in an inelegant heap toward her. She rolls away with a screech like a wildcat, as if it's *my* fault I was about to crush her.

"Valor."

I push myself up from the frozen ground onto my elbows. Immaculate gray boots come into my field of vision. I raise my head.

"Proclivities for violence will not be tolerated here," says Warden Kirov.

"But I wasn't— I didn't mean to—"

"This is not a good start, Valor."

The rest of the line ahead of me has disappeared into the building, including the girl. I haul myself to my feet, but Warden Kirov is already walking away.

Nothing I do or say means the same as it did before. I was the daughter of two of the queen's highest-ranking officials. Now I'm nothing more than a traitor and a prisoner. I brush myself off and follow through the narrow doorway into a long hall. Thick ice blocks rise, translucent and shimmering, to a roof of pink-hued ice reflecting the dawn sky.

At one end of the room there's a counter with a man behind it, serving something that smells like salty porridge in wooden bowls. Down the length of the room are wooden tables with stools bolted along either side. Most of them are filled already with boys and girls. I stand and stare until my stomach drives me forward with a loud gurgling that reminds me I haven't eaten since Feliks offered me a date under the cart in the market. He was right; I should have taken more.

I walk the length of the hall, searching every face. The girl I accidentally tripped scowls at me. I skip over my cellmate, trying to ignore how annoyed I am with her for not telling me what was going to happen. It wouldn't have hurt her to explain. As I walk, I can't help but notice that a lot of the faces are staring back at me. No, not at me, exactly—at my head. I wipe my hand across my forehead and my fingers come away with a trace of gritty ink on them. They're staring at the ink mark. And I can't see Sasha anywhere.

At the counter, I feel eyes on me as I walk along to collect my food. The man behind the metal vat hands me a bowl, his hands tattooed front and back with human eyes. Black-inked wolves snarl and fight all the way up his arms. The food barely covers the bottom of the bowl, and now I understand how the warden manages to get three hundred children out of their bunks and into this hall with only a handful of Peacekeepers around. If we don't get here in time, we don't eat.

I turn around, hoping to find a different route back along the hall, but a sea of downturned faces meets me, and I see no spaces apart from two that have magically materialized on either side of my sour-looking cellmate. They must think I'm her burden to bear. She looks as though she would as soon kill me with her spoon, but there's nowhere else to sit, and besides, Feliks is sitting on the stool opposite her.

I'm so glad to see his still-dirty face that I smile as I take my sorry self and my sorry bowl over to sit by my cellmate. Feliks doesn't smile back. My cellmate has a full bowl, like everyone else at the table.

The Peacekeeper with the chessboard tattoos stands in one corner of the hall, and Peacekeeper Rurik is in the corner diagonal to him. They look like statues in the ghostly light inside the ice hall.

"Feliks," I say. "I'm sorry for what—"

He cuts me off with a little jerk of his hand. "Keep your voice down. Do you want to cause more trouble? We've only been here five minutes."

There are a few mutterings and glances from around the table. My cellmate is staring with undisguised horror at Feliks's grubby face. There are two boys wearing patched furs tucking into their food with alarming speed. A girl with black hair looks away when I catch her eye.

I touch the mark on my head. It's dried onto my skin. Feliks glances behind him and says in a voice barely louder than the falling of snow, "You've broken one of the rules already—probably the one about doing what everybody else does when everybody else does it."

"I don't think that's one of the rules, Feliks. And if it is, nobody told me. Even though they could have."

My cellmate's spoon pauses briefly on its way to her mouth, and then she carries on.

Feliks makes a tiny shrug. "I'm not the one with the mark on my head, am I? I intend to do what everyone else does when everyone else does it." He gives a little nod as though he's confirming it to himself, though maybe he's telling everyone else at the table that he's not like me. He's not. Nobody here is. Everyone is dressed in dirty rags, and I still have my fine hunting gear on. I'm doubly out of place.

I bend my head to the pitiful amount of food in my bowl and spoon it into my mouth in three bites. It's salty and lumpy and the whole hall smells like pig swill because of it, but oh, how I wish there was more.

"I'm not going to do anything else wrong," I say. "But I need to find my sister. Have any—"

"Will you both," says my cellmate, eyeing the Peace-keeper nearest us, "shut up, before *Valor* here gets another infraction."

I've been awake for two days. I've had practically nothing to eat for that whole time, unless you count a date and an inch of slop, which I do not. And I have not found my sister. The way my cellmate says my name is the last feather on an arrow that's already snapped. I leap to my feet, banging my calf on the iron bar affixing the stool to the table.

"Clearly you don't care, and nothing I can say is going to make you, but *some* of us come from good families who we care about and who care about us."

She stares up at me without moving, eyes furious, mouth in a pinched line, and I feel total satisfaction at how angry she is for about three seconds before the red eyes of Peacekeeper Rurik's demon tattoo appear right above me.

I sink down onto my stool like a dead bird falling from the sky. But he reaches for the pouch around his waist anyway. There's audible grumbling as I get a second line of ink on my forehead.

"No roof tonight," Rurik's voice rumbles out, echoing a little off the ice. "Stand up for work assignments."

Everyone stands behind their stool in silence. I do the same, trying not to look at the narrowed eyes directed at me. No roof tonight? He can't mean that they expect us to sleep in our cells with no roof on the cellblock, can he?

I can't stop thinking about it as the room is divided into work details—some to the kitchens, some to the laundry or the forge, some to maintenance of the ice buildings, and some to the mines. Since the jobs are handed out in blocks, I'm sent to work in the mines with Feliks. And my cellmate.

As we file out of the ice hall, Feliks pushes up close to me and says, "Your cellmate—I heard her name is Katia. And if we all *have* to work together, you should stop making her angry."

And just how am I supposed to do that? I think. But I say nothing, because she's right in front of me. The sun is bright outside, and the temperature has risen a few degrees. A small group of prisoners is walking from the cellblock almost directly toward us. I shade my eyes from the glare of the sun on the snow. They're a ragtag bunch with Peacekeepers both ahead of and behind them.

As the first Peacekeeper passes, I keep my eyes to the front, ignoring the explosion of tattoos covering him. I don't dare think what will happen if I get a third infraction.

"Mine detail, this way," calls a tall prisoner. Katia immediately changes direction, and as I follow, a boy from the other group walks past me. Behind him I see a brown *ushanka*, and then everything slows down and speeds up at the same time. Under the hat is a face as familiar to me as my own. Her brown eyes go wide and her mouth falls open, and then she's gone before I can even get a sound out.

Sasha.

A shot of energy races through my body and speeds my heart up, even though she's already disappeared, blocked by the Peacekeeper behind her.

I keep my boots moving through the snow until we near the face of the white cliff, but my head is spinning, and my heart pounds as though I'm on a hunt for a rogue wolf. A million little memories blast into my head—Sasha crying when I cried, laughing when I laughed. Sasha annoyed when one of my arrows ripped her favorite skirt; Sasha sneaking cake out of the kitchen and up to my room when I was being punished and should have had none.

The prisoner boy at the head of our line calls out a halt, then starts barking orders. We stand in loose formation while he talks. I can't listen to a word he says.

"Feliks!" I whisper without turning my head. "Did you see her? That was my sister. She's here." The relief buzzing through me is incredible. I hadn't let myself think that something might have happened to her, but now that I've seen her I know, deep inside, I was so scared it had.

For a second, I don't think Feliks is even going to talk to me again, but then he pretends to adjust his boot and glances after the little group, which is just heading into the ice hall now. "Why is she with them?"

I glance sidelong at Katia. She isn't angry anymore. Some other expression is on her face.

"What is it?" I ask. Suddenly I feel a bit dizzy, a bit sick. That look on her face is half pity.

She presses her lips together, considering whether to answer me at all.

"Please," I say.

She sighs a puff of white into the air. "They're called the Black Hands. All the most dangerous prisoners, kept away from the rest of us. They always have Peacekeepers with them. You won't be able to talk to her."

There's a buzzing in my ears, and Feliks nudges me. "Face the front, Valor. You're going to get us all in trouble."

CHAPTER 7

I do what he says, but I only stare numbly, even after the group starts moving toward an opening in the cliff. I've finally found my sister, and I can't speak to her. And if I can't even speak to her, how can I break her out?

The sheer face rises almost vertically from the ground behind the buildings of Tyur'ma. The walls of the fortress tower on either side, and the peak of the mountain disappears into the mist far above us. As we near the entrance to the mine, the rock sparkles slightly. There are seams of minerals streaked through it in delicate shades of green.

A great fissure runs from high above my head, widening down to the ground. There are torches on both sides of the opening, and as we pass through into the mine, my brain starts to thaw. The thrill of seeing Sasha was so brief and bittersweet—but at least she's alive. I see her shocked face over and over again in my mind. All the words I need to say to her mound up in my head like snowdrifts.

The torchlight is dim in the cave. Tall prisoner boy stands in front of us again, issuing more instructions, but I can't focus on what he's saying.

I realize I'd been expecting to swoop into Tyur'ma, find my sister, and heroically rescue her. Now I find she's separated from the rest of us. And every second she's in here, she's with the most dangerous prisoners Tyur'ma has. Something's wrong. Since when is stealing a music box— even such an important one—*dangerous*?

A sharp pain in my shin jolts me out of my thoughts. Feliks is staring at me expectantly with wide eyes. He has an unlit torch in one hand and a small leather bag in the other. I look around and see Katia and the rest of the group taking pickaxes and other tools from a rack against the wall of the cave. There's a Peacekeeper standing by it, watching us. Feliks is right. I have to start paying attention.

I join my group—five boys and five girls, including me and Katia—and choose a canvas bag full of heavy, clanking tools from the rack. There's a stack of torches in an iron-bound barrel, and I grab one. I fall into line, and we take turns lighting our small torches on the larger ones by the entrance. Katia's face is lit warm orange as she holds her torch to the flame and waits for it to catch. There are freckles across her pale skin that I hadn't noticed before.

As the last of each group ignites their torches, light flares around the cave, throwing shadows all over a cavern that I now see stretches deep into the cliff. We're standing on a plateau, and below us is a huge, echoing space hewn out of the white rock. Several dark tunnels snake off from it into the mountain.

"It smells old," says Feliks.

It's true. The air is cold and dry. The cliff must have been here for eons. It makes me feel like we shouldn't be in here, tiny humans picking away at its insides with our sharp tools.

The prisoner boy in charge holds his torch high. "You five, this way. The rest of you will be working down that shaft. The spaces are too small for a Peacekeeper, so Katia will be in charge while you're working." He looks straight at me. "And for those of you who may not have been paying attention, my name is Nicolai." I panic, heat rushing up my cheeks, wondering if he can hand out infractions too. But if I'm not mistaken, he's actually smiling. A tiny smile, not meant for anyone else to see, but still a smile.

I watch him lead the other group down to the tunnel. He's about the same height as Katia, but his eyes and hair are dark, like mine. He doesn't look any older than me, though. I turn to ask Katia about him, but she's standing with the rest of our group behind her, her arms crossed and an unamused expression on her face.

"I'm sorry," I say. "Please. Lead on."

"Oh, thank you *so* much for your permission." She shoots off down a narrow tunnel with the others behind her.

Our torches light the white walls, and the seams of green glitter in the rock as we pass. I think about Nicolai, about him being in charge of the mine detail. He must have earned that responsibility somehow.

I'm cut off from my train of thought by a green glow ahead. The tunnel opens up, and Katia, at the head of the line, carries her torch into a cave. The rest of the group file through—two girls, then Feliks and me.

Feliks stares with his mouth open, his broken tooth on show.

"It's some kind of mineral," I tell him. The cave has been expanded by previous miners until it looks like the inside of a geode my father kept on his desk. Around us, the formations of rock glow in the torchlight in every shade of green, from new spring leaf to deep moss. Swirling circular patterns burst one next to the other, covering the wall and roof in a mass of texture and color.

Katia drops her tools to the floor with a clang. Feliks and I follow suit, opening our bags to reveal picks and axes and small metal tools with sharp hooks and blades.

"Since I'm certain some of us weren't listening," says Katia, "this mineral is malachite. It's rare, it's valuable, and it's in great demand by rich folk to make into jewelry and inlay their fancy tables. For you new people, you might think this is easy with no Peacekeeper here, but you're wrong. We have to produce a certain amount of it by the end of the shift, and they'll be checking. And there's nowhere to go but dead ends and unstable mine shafts in here, so don't even think about it." She shows us how to use the tools, then abruptly turns her back and starts to work.

Feliks and I look at each other, and then I hand him one of the silver tools. He sighs and hands me a pickax. Within minutes my hands start to blister, though I'm no stranger to work. I hope Sasha hasn't been in here. She's not as strong as I am.

"Why is she with them at all?" I wonder, then realize I said it out loud. Surely it should be me, not Sasha, placed with them after what I've done.

"What?" One of the girls stops swinging her pickax. Her face shines with sweat, and her hands are wide and strong.

"Nothing," I say. Then I realize this might be my only chance to ask the question without a Peacekeeper over-hearing. "Do you know why a girl whose only crime was theft would be with the group they keep separate? The Black Hands?"

The girl's lip curls. "Maybe she's like you—a trouble-maker. Couldn't keep your mouth shut, could you? Had to earn another infraction."

"Leave her alone. She can't help it," says Feliks.

My gaze snaps to him in surprise. I cough to cover up the little rush of gratitude I feel.

"Natalia, back to work," says Katia sharply. "Work that seam along there." She points to a crevice at the back of the cave. The girl gives me a filthy look and does as she says.

I look at Feliks and Katia. I should distance myself from them. Everyone hates me. I still have the ink marks on my head, and until they're gone I have no hope of that changing.

I tell myself I'm not here to make friends.

"I can look after myself," I say to Katia. I start picking up my tools so I can move away. I know she gave that order simply to get the work done, not to speak up for me, but I don't want to seem like I need the help.

As I step away, though, Feliks gathers his things too, standing up with the pickax.

"What are you doing? You should stay by Katia," I mumble.

"You too good for help when it's offered?" he asks in a low voice. "You can barely pay attention as it is. I'm sorry you can't talk to your sister, but we have a quota to meet. Didn't you hear Nicolai?" He looks straight at the ground. "Look—about before. You know, when you . . . I'm not stupid. I know what would have happened if you hadn't stopped me trying to escape. I owe you." He tilts his face up, looking determined.

Katia clears her throat. "You both need to get to work there," she says gruffly. "I'm stuck with you as a cellmate, Valor, whether I like it or not. And Feliks is right, we have to get the work done."

A few seconds pass before I can speak, and even then my voice is wobbly. "Katia, I'm sorry for what I said at breakfast."

She doesn't acknowledge the apology, but as we turn back to our work, I'm still glad I said it. We work in silence for a few minutes, and then Katia says without looking at me, "Your sister's boots are as fine as yours. How did two girls like you end up in here?" She eyes my clothes. "Unless, of course, you stole it all. But no common thief gets herself into the Black Hands."

"I'm not a thief," I say cautiously. This is the most Katia's said to me so far. "And my sister is not a criminal. Not really."

Katia barks a laugh. "She says she didn't do it? She has that in common with almost everyone else in here, then. Do you think this place works on fairness? Look at Nicolai. Only been here a month, and he's giving out orders already."

I take a chisel and smash it into the rock, though it burns the blisters I am sure cover every inch of my hands under my mittens. "Would you consider a thirteen-year-old girl who stole a music box to be dangerous?"

A flicker of curiosity passes over her face, but she shrugs. I remember the way she twitched in the dining hall when she heard Feliks ask about my sister. "Do . . . *you* have a sister, Katia? Or a brother? Sasha shouldn't be with the Black Hands. I have to speak to her. I have to—"

"You have to get back to work is what you have to do." Her voice is clipped and closed off. The conversation is over.

When my stomach rumbles and my arms feel weak and numb from hefting the pickax, I glance at Feliks to see if he's doing any better than I am. He's fallen asleep. I steal a quick look at Katia to see if she's noticed, then reach out to shake him awake. I don't want him getting in trouble after what he said earlier.

"I haven't seen him," Katia says. She stops her work, breathing hard, but doesn't turn around.

"What?"

"If I see him, I have to report him." She wipes the back of her hand across her face. "So don't make me turn around."

There's a little quiet, and I feel like I have to say something. "Thanks."

"I'm not doing it for you." She's taken her coat off, and underneath her clothes are rough and patched, nothing like the finely woven tunic I'm wearing. Her shoulders drop and she sighs, as though she's debating something inside. "They keep the Black Hands in the isolation cells."

"What?" I'm immediately focused. Natalia glances over, sees Feliks, and deliberately turns away. I lower my voice anyway. "Where are they?"

"I'll show you later, when we go back to the cellblock."

I want to question her until she's given up every bit of information she knows, but I don't let myself in case she changes her mind.

As Katia returns to work, I lean over Feliks and pull his furs closer around him. While I'm doing it, I take one of the smallest picks and push it up my sleeve. It's metal, which means it can be melted down. I hesitate for a second, thinking about Feliks and Katia and even Natalia, about the infractions I've already earned, and then I slip it into the hidden compartment on the side of my boot. I need my own set of keys to my cell if any of my plans are going to work.

The moon hangs low and heavy when we stand again in the entrance of the mine. My back aches, and my hands are weak and throbbing from the work. Feliks stumbles to the rack to return the bag of tools. Nicolai stops him, his face tired in the orange light from a brazier. There's a Peacekeeper behind him.

"Tool check."

The other prisoners fall into line behind us, but suddenly I am wide awake again, fresh sweat pricking my back. Nicolai sorts through the bag and frowns.

Stupid. I am so stupid. I'm not in a world where trust exists anymore. Of course there would be a count.

"One broke," I blurt out. "A very small pick."

"Where are the pieces?" Nicolai looks from me to Katia.

Katia stands straight. "I don't have them. She didn't report it."

"I . . ." My mind is blank. I have nothing.

"It was destroyed," says Feliks, "when the transport cart ran over it. But there are probably some splinters left. I could go back and find them." Behind us, the other prisoners shift, one of them muttering something inaudible. They're tired and hungry. We all are.

Nicolai looks hard at all three of us. "That won't be necessary, inmate."

I start to breathe again.

"But I'll need to search you all." He points at Feliks and me. "Starting with you two."

I stand rigid, vividly aware of the compartment in my boot.

Feliks steps forward and Nicolai checks under his collar, all over his clothing, and even makes him take his boots off. My heart thuds loud enough for him to hear. "Katia," Nicolai says, making me jump. "Search this inmate." Katia comes forward, searching me all over while I hold my breath.

"She's clean," she says in a cold, sullen voice.

"Go," Nicolai says to me. And I do.

There's a meal of bread, cheese, and milk that I all but inhale, and then we're separated, boys from girls, and marched back to the cellblock by a Peacekeeper with magnificent eagles carrying skulls tattooed across her arms. On either side of her shoulders, huge black wingtips poke out from under her clothes. She must have a giant eagle across the entirety of her broad back.

The only thing keeping me from falling asleep on my feet is the promise of what Katia might tell me. And as we file through the narrow doorway into the cellblock, I hear a voice in my ear. It's her. "Look up."

I stop myself from turning toward her and drawing attention. I look down the length of the cellblock at the rows of cells, and up to the roof, open to the dusky sky. A pale moon is partially obscured by wisps of cloud.

"At the back, after the third level, there's another set of steps cut into the wall. Can you see them?"

She's talking low and fast. I try to slow the line down, dragging my feet. I can just make out some sharply ascending steps set high up, leading to a narrow crack in the stone. "I see them."

"There are cells at the top of those steps. That's where

she'll be. Now you know. And there's nothing you can do about it, so don't ask me for anything else."

I shake my head. There's no room for cells up there. But Katia's already gone.

"Move along," calls the Peacekeeper. "You. Wait there." She pulls me aside and waits until all the other girls have scurried up or down the steps. When everyone is inside their cell, the screeching noise of the doors being rolled shut starts. My heart pounds in my ears along with the grate of metal on stone. When it ends and the cells are locked in position, the Peacekeeper marches me down the steps to the lower level, her boots scraping the stone in the sudden silence.

There's only darkness in the cells, the prisoners already in their bunks. Torches flare at intervals on the walls. I'm led to the middle of the floor, each second that ticks by winding my muscles tighter. The Peacekeeper leans down, and I suck in a breath at the snarling snow leopard inked on the back of her arm, haunches bunched as though it might leap from her skin to destroy me.

The chains at her waist clink, and I see she's running them through an iron ring embedded in the stone floor. When she stands, she's holding cuffs like the ones Feliks and I wore on our way here. I force myself to hold out my arms. There is no point in making this worse—if it *can* be any worse. The Peacekeeper shackles me, the cold iron weighting my wrists. I shiver as she drops the chains to the floor with an echoing rattle and walks away. Her footsteps move up the stone stairs, and the iron door clangs.

The cellblock is silent. I sink down to the ground, the heavy chain sliding into a noisy pile with me. A bunk in the row to the left of me creaks.

"If you're still alive in the morning, you'll wish you'd been quiet tonight," a voice hisses at me. I swallow. Above us, the stars are coming out in a cold, clear night. That's when the muttering starts, whispering from the cells, and the reality of what I've done hits me. They're not going to roll the roof over us tonight. Everyone is going to be cold, and it's only going to get colder. I have to stay out here all night on my own, with no bed. And it's all my fault.

Any trouble my sister or I have been in before feels like nothing now. Back when we were nine, we were once in the palace kitchens while our mother and the queen were discussing a problem. The queen and the princess had been overseeing preparations for a banquet.

As the three of us stood dutifully, listening to our mothers, Sasha inched her fingers backward to a table, closed them around a little pastry, and fed it into her pocket. Not five minutes later, one of the cooks was blaming the theft on a little kitchen girl, who was denying it at such a high pitch that the queen strode across the kitchen to deal with the matter herself.

Sasha was wide-eyed, breathing fast. She stepped forward and reached for her pocket. I stepped with her. But then Anastasia reached up and touched her mother's arm. She told the whole kitchen in a clear voice that she had meant no harm, hadn't realized that it would matter, had only seen how pretty the pastries were and wanted one for herself.

I think about that day as I sit, my fingers starting to go numb. There's no one here to help Sasha now but me. I look up, high on the far wall, at the opening in the rock that Katia showed me. There's no way to get there from the ground floor. I'll have to go back up the steps, past the door to the cellblock, then to the next level and along the ledge right past my own cell and all the others to get to the steps to the isolation cells. I'm so tired that just the thought of it seems too much. But at least there are no Peacekeepers inside the cellblock.

I huddle in on myself, careful to keep the chains quiet. I don't need anyone seeing what I'm going to do. The cuffs clink together a little as I work the tool I stole out of my boot. I meant for it to be melted down to help me make the keys I need, but maybe I can use it for something else too. I can still melt it down later.

It takes a few seconds to work one of my mittens off and twist the sharp end of the pick into the lock. My fingers are shaking and sore, raw with the cold and the work they've done today in the mines.

Every time I slip, someone curses me and the small noises I'm making. I'm almost ready to give up. But then something gives in the lock mechanism, and one of the cuffs springs open. I rub my wrist, flexing my fingers. There's no movement from the cells closest to me. If their days have been anything like mine, they're exhausted and, I hope, asleep. The other cuff gives quickly now that I know what I'm doing. I place the chains on the cold ground, listen for a moment, and then stand. I take one step.

"What do you think you're doing?" a low voice snarls at me from a darkened cell. "If you make it two nights with no roof, you won't live to see a third."

I look at the stone steps. "If *you* tell anyone what I'm doing, then you *will* have two nights with no roof. And maybe worse." I've never heard my own voice come out like that before. I hope it sounded fierce, not desperate. I take another step, my heart leaping up into my throat. The cell is silent.

I go and listen at the iron door. It's silent on the other side; only my own breath sounds loud in my ears. Dim torchlight throws flickering shadows over the steps Katia showed me. This could be what I've been waiting for. I summon up my last reserve of energy and head for them.

The stone path up to the first level seems so much narrower than it did this morning when I flew down the steps away from the Peacekeeper. As I creep along the ledge outside the cells, some of the girls inside stare at me tight-lipped, and some call out horrible things. I take care that my furs don't brush the bars of each cell, trying not to even breathe.

I near the back of the room and catch sight of something flying toward me out of the corner of my eye. I flinch away from it, but not fast enough. Freezing water slaps me in the face, and I gasp, stumbling toward the edge where the stone drops away to the open ground below.

I teeter on the brink, sure I'm going to fall, but I'm grabbed by an arm and yanked back onto the ledge. I yell, my heart beating wildly, and pull away from the grip on me, but I soon realize that without the girl reaching out across the ledge from her cell, I'd be broken on the ground by now, maybe even dead.

I take a big, shaky breath. "Thank you."

She lets go of my arm and nods. There's a black patch over one of her eyes. "Everyone deserves a chance," she says, her voice surprisingly low. "You in there, back away and let her pass." There's grumbling, then movement in the cell next door.

I shiver, thin, icy fingers of water trickling down my neck. "Will the Peacekeepers come back?"

"Not at night—unless someone gives them a reason to. The cells are locked, and even if they weren't, the cellblock is locked too." The girl with the eye patch gives me another nod. "Go on now." She raises her voice. "No one else will bother you."

A girl glowers from the back of her cell as I pass, and my heart keeps up its frantic beat while I climb the next flight of stairs to the top level. Now I'm standing right by the steep steps Katia pointed out, and I start to wonder if it was some cruel joke. I'm so tired; my thoughts flit around, and it's hard to pin them in place. I haul myself up to the first step and push my feet onto it, not looking down, knowing that there's only air between me and a drop that would surely kill me.

As I climb, I keep my eyes on the crevice in the stone as if there's a rope attached to it, pulling me forward, and when I reach the top, I slide into the gap and let out a sob. The sky lightens above me, and slow, fat flakes of snow start to fall.

"Who's there?"

I start at the sound of the voice, and then edge forward into the opening in the wall and around a corner. There's a small row of cells open to the sky. A face presses against the first set of bars, the whites of its eyes showing. Filthy hands wrapped in rags clasp the bars. I put my finger to my lips.

Dark shapes huddle in the next two cells. I press against the far wall to pass by. Opposite the fourth cell, I stop. Inside sits a slightly built girl, shivering even though she's covered in brown furs.

"Sasha." I whisper her name and run to her, dropping to my knees, not caring about the cold or the snow or the bars between us. It doesn't matter what anyone here or in the city thinks of me or what I've done. It was all worth it. I press my arms through the gaps to hug her, and she does the same. My face is pushed into cold, hard iron, and I don't care at all.

"Valor!" she says. "How are you here?" Her voice is full of disbelief, but her arms are so tight around me it hurts.

Snowflakes flurry around us, settling on my furs before melting.

I hug her back just as hard. "I'm so sorry, Sasha. I should never have talked on and on the way I did about the parade. I should have realized. I should have stopped you. But I have a plan. I have a plan, Sasha, and I'm going to get you out of here." I pull back finally and look at her. "We're going to escape."

She takes hold of my wrists and looks at me wonderingly. Tears shine in her eyes. "What are you talking about? How did you even get here? You have to go before someone sees you. We can't escape. And what do you mean, you should have stopped me? Stopped me from what?"

I search her face. She's perhaps a little thinner than before, but her eyes are as bright and full of intelligence as ever. It feels like there's a date pit stuck in my throat that I have to swallow away.

"From stealing the music box, of course. But I'm going to make it up to you. Don't you see? Now I've found you, and we're going to figure out how to get you out of here." I grab the bars of her cell and tug on them. "And once you're out with the rest of us, I have a plan. I found a way on Father's secret maps and memorized it. I'm going to get keys. We can escape, Sasha. It will work, it *will*."

She shakes her head. "Secret maps? I don't— I didn't—"

"You've never seen them?"

"Not the ones you speak of, but I can believe it. There are hidden passageways in the palace itself." She shakes her head again, and her face clears as she looks at me. "I thought I'd never see you again," she whispers. Then her brows crease, and she peers anxiously down the narrow corridor. "But you must go. What about Mother and Father? Do they know what you're . . . ? I can't believe you're here. I can't believe what you're saying. But, Valor, I didn't steal the music box."

I stare. My cheeks burn. For seconds, I can't speak.

I didn't believe she was guilty at first, of course. None of us did. But there was no choice after the evidence was presented. It's only now that I realize how fully I'd begun to accept it as truth. Then I was so busy planning to get myself in here, I didn't think about it at all anymore.

I suppose I didn't want to.

Sasha pulls back. "You thought I stole it?" She stops glancing nervously down the corridor and leans back, wrapping her arms around her knees.

"I . . . I'm sorry. I thought . . . we all thought . . ."

Her head lifts, eyes sparking with understanding.

Suddenly, I couldn't feel any worse. What was I thinking, believing in anything but my sister?

Sasha's expression softens. "Don't apologize. It's what you were supposed to think. I've been wondering why I'm locked up here away from everyone else." She climbs up onto her knees. "They keep me with the Black Hands, Valor. I don't speak to anyone else."

I shake my head, too tired to follow her thoughts and too sorry that I'd trusted the system of justice even up until this moment. I should never have trusted anything over my sister. It seems so obvious now.

"If no one knows I didn't steal the music box, not even Mother and Father . . ." She waves her hand, beckoning me on to the realization. It used to drive me insane when she did that, waiting for me to catch up. "No one asks the question . . . ?"

"Who *did* steal the music box?" I finish.

CHAPTER 8

She speaks fast, her face pressed to the bars. "Yes, who? And why? Obviously whoever it was needed somebody to blame. And I'm it."

"So that's why you couldn't tell anyone where the box was—because you never knew?"

Sasha nods, then her gaze drops and fixes on the bars. "You really never considered I might be innocent?" She looks up again, and I can barely meet her eye.

I shrug helplessly. How can I even begin to explain that I'd just grown to accept that she had taken the box? My voice comes out soft, soaked in misery. "I didn't care whether you'd done it or not. I'd have come for you no matter what you'd done. But you'd been seen so many times trying to gain access to the box. There were witnesses. And you had no alibi, and . . . the evidence was very convincing . . ." I trail off, shame-faced.

She swallows, and I see her do something she's done before. On the day my sister was due to be introduced to Father's colleagues as his apprentice, one of the princess's ponies fell badly. The groomsman had no choice but to shoot the poor beast. It was the pony Sasha always rode when she accompanied the princess on rides, and both girls cried bitterly, clinging to each other.

Sasha knew our father would have allowed her to delay her apprenticeship by one day. But she also knew how it would look if the queen's future adviser couldn't put her own concerns away for the good of the realm. She dried her tears and pressed her lips together and put on her new uniform in her bedroom while I sat on her bed wanting to do something to help.

I see that same look on her face now as she narrows her eyes at the ground, still thinking. "Yes, it was very convincing. Whoever wanted me to look guilty did an excellent job of it."

I curl close against the bars, tugging my mittens up under my sleeves as she thinks. I start to shiver, the cold and the reality of where we are seeping into me.

"Oh, saints, are you cold? Of course you are. Here." Sasha feeds half her blanket through the bars to cover me, though I can barely focus on what's happening anymore. I have never been so tired in my entire life, and I doubt I could recite my own name were someone to ask me for it. The snow stops, and the stars come out again. They're the last things I see as I drift off, holding tight to my sister's mitten-covered hands through the bars.

I wake with a start, stiff with cold. I'm still clutching Sasha's hands. The sky is dove white, and there are puddles of slush around us. It's morning. I don't know how I can have slept for so long. Sasha stirs, moving her hands away from mine.

"You let me sleep?"

"I had no choice," she says. "I couldn't wake you." Then she blinks, and her usual sharp, focused expression returns. "You have to get back down there before the cells open. Run." Her breath freezes in the air, and she's shivering.

I push the blanket back into her cell and stand up slowly, feeling like I'm frozen almost solid. "I meant everything I said, Sasha. We're getting out of here."

I want to say more. I want to tell her how sorry I am and how wrong I was and that I can't believe I let myself get taken in by evidence that someone fabricated.

She puts her arms through the bars, and I hug her tight. "It should have been me, of all people, who knew you were innocent," I say. "I'm sorry."

I feel her nod against my neck, and then I turn away, heading back out through the passage in the stone. I should feel worse than I do, chilled to the bone, hungry, and still tired. I should be terrified that I'm going to get caught. But all I can think about as I hurry away is that I did it. I found Sasha. And now there's nothing I won't do to get her out of Tyur'ma.

I force my cold, clumsy feet down the steps, level after level, until I'm standing by my cell.

"You're still alive. How did you get out of those chains?" Katia stands rigid at the cell door, waiting for it to open. She doesn't sound too disappointed, and I choose to take that as a good sign.

"You were right about where my sister was," I say. But before I have a chance to say anything else, the cell doors start rolling back. I run for the lower level where I should still be chained, my heart bursting into such a fast rhythm that it hurts. I snatch up the chains, huddling over them and trying to calm my breathing. My stiff fingers won't move fast enough.

The Peacekeeper reaches me seconds after I snap the manacles back into place, and I wait for her to notice, wait for her to see how fast my icy breath comes. Then, as she unshackles me, I wait for one of the other inmates to give me away.

But they stand silent, shivering in their cells, the threat of another night with no roof keeping them quiet. The Peacekeeper barely looks at me. And this time, when the rolling of the doors stops, I know what's going to happen, and I ready myself to take my place in the crowd and run the minute the rush starts.

∽⟋⟍∽

Today I get a full bowl of the oaty mixture they call breakfast. I do my best to ignore the looks of hatred from the frozen girls and take my seat by Feliks and Katia. We're told that we'll be working in the laundry today.

When we line up in our groups, I find that Natalia, Nicolai, and the others who were with him are in our detail again. The laundry is a long trek back past our cellblock. We continue to another block, and Feliks leans forward to whisper that this is where he sleeps. There are other smaller buildings. I smell heat and hear the clanking of metal from one of them—it's a forge of some kind. I went to one once with my mother, and she showed me how they made the weapons we used for hunting. She wanted me to know every part of the job I was to assume, right down to an understanding of the skill it takes to make a hunting knife, a sword, or an arrowhead.

I see her face in my mind, glowing with the heat of the fires in the forge as she explained how the molds and the heat shaped the metal. I feel the sparks on my skin, smell the iron and the soft leather of my mother's clothing. Her hair was braided into one thick tress. She never had the patience to sit and put the customary number of braids in, or to loop them as the rest of the women of the hunt did.

The chill wind blows the warmth of the memory away. I pull my coat closer against it. Feliks shivers as we walk past the forge. His hand moves to his arm, rubbing at it, and there's a strange look on his face. I remember something he said back in the palace dungeon, something about him being an apprentice.

"Have you been in a forge before?" I ask.

His eyes dart to me, and he nods. "Worked in one for a while after my parents died. Didn't really suit me." He walks off ahead, and then we're called to a halt and I don't get the chance to ask more.

The laundry is a long building, two stories high. It sits right in front of a circular tower that stands in the corner against both cliff and wall and reaches up as high as the walls. There's a tiny slit of a window at the top of the tower, and movement catches my eye. Someone's watching us.

I'm knocked forward as Natalia shoulders me out of the way. One of the others has slipped and fallen. Natalia hauls the boy to his feet and roughly brushes the snow from his furs.

When I look at the tower again, there's nobody there.

"Come on, Valor," says Feliks.

As soon as I get inside the doors of the laundry, I know that no better detail could have been handed out to our group today. The Peacekeeper shuts the doors and takes up a stance by them, and I let the heat wash over me, relaxing my muscles. Steam rises from stout wooden vats along the walls. Each tub is chained to iron pegs sunk into the floor. In the center of the room there are slatted wooden steps that lead up to the second floor. The air smells of soap and warmth.

"This way," says Katia. She leads us into a side room, and I wrinkle my nose. In the room is a mountain of under-clothes, trousers, and tunics. Everything each prisoner wears under their furs. And it looks as though every single prisoner has changed their clothes today.

"Dig in. This happens only once every two weeks. You'll have to wait for clean things, though—we do half the inmates one week and half the next." Katia sounds positively cheer-ful, although I'd rather skin a stag than touch anything in here. We take our coats off and each grab an armful of the laundry, dumping it into the vats of soapy water. My hands sting when I reach into the warmth to start scrubbing, but soon Feliks, Katia, and I are hard at work wrangling sopping-wet clothing.

Nicolai is farther down the room, his head bent over the mound of clothes he's scrubbing. Natalia and another prisoner are opposite, twisting white sheets to wring water from them. The other prisoner is small, and Natalia's doing most of the work, making sure the sheet doesn't drag on the floor. I watch her smile a little and shake her head as her partner struggles.

"Where are those sheets from?" I ask.

"Who cares about sheets?" says Feliks.

I look to Katia. Her face is closed. She scrubs hard at something woollen. Water slops out onto the floor and runs down underneath the tub. There must be a drain under there.

"Katia, where are they from?"

"The hospital block. Why?"

"I'll be back in a minute," I say. I shoot up the stairs to the second level. As I thought, there are lines strung all over the place, the laundry drying in the heat rising from the washtubs. I tear down a white sheet and fold it as small as I can before jamming it into the waistband of my trousers. Then I shuffle the rest of the laundry along so there's no gap and race back down the stairs.

"What are you doing now?" Katia says with a frown.

"Just checking how much space is left up there," I say.

I carry on working until the steam mixes in beads with the sweat on my face, but I watch the rest of the group at their stations, waiting for everyone's attention to be elsewhere. I glance at the Peacekeeper. He stands like a statue by the door, not watching me. I slip a bar of soap into my pocket. I'll need it to make impressions of the keys I'm going to steal. When I turn back, Katia's sleeves are rolled up to her elbows and her arms are dripping. But her eyes are on me, and her mouth is a rigid line. She saw me.

"What are you *doing*?" Her voice is a low, furious whisper. Feliks looks between me and Katia, his eyes wary.

"If you're caught stealing, we'll all be punished. *Again.*"

I shake my head, trying to think of something to say.

She lowers her voice even further. "Put it back. Put it back right now before someone sees."

"What's going on?" asks Feliks.

Katia bends over the washtub again, scrubbing extra hard, her jaw clamped shut.

"Shh," I say. I have to keep the rising fear out of my voice.

"Why should he be quiet?" Katia asks. "In fact, why should *I*? I felt sorry for you; I *tried* to help you, but why *shouldn't* we inform on you? If anyone else had seen you, they'd do it in a heartbeat. And then they'd get the reward."

"What reward?" asks Feliks.

I scrub the clothes in front of me, hardly seeing what I'm doing. I have to say something. She *has* to keep quiet. But I need this soap too. I might not have another chance to get some, and I'm not putting it back.

I cast a glance around. No one's listening. I lock eyes with Katia and keep my voice low. "Listen," I say, moving around the tub so that I'm closer to her. "I have a plan." My skin prickles despite the warmth. If Katia won't listen or, worse, if she tells anyone, I'll never get Sasha out of here. I can't live with any more guilt than what's already piled on top of me.

"What sort of plan?" asks Feliks.

I suck in a breath. "The sort that ends with us on the other side of that wall, far away from here, without anybody realizing we're gone."

They both stop what they're doing and stare.

Katia shakes her head. "Don't even *think* about escaping. There's no point in tormenting yourself. Just accept your fate."

"I make my own fate. You'll see. Keep working," I whisper.

But Feliks grins at me. I hadn't planned on taking anyone else when we escape, but I can't very well leave him now. I remember holding on to him as he struggled to run away from Peacekeeper Rurik. I still wonder whether he could have gotten away if I'd let him go. Katia, however, is a different matter. "Katia, my father had old maps of the city. Just listen to what I have—"

"No, *you* listen," she says. "I've seen people try to escape before. I've seen girls shot down before they even made it to the wall and left on the ground for two days with arrows in their backs and their blood soaking into the snow. I even saw one girl make it to the wall. She'd found some way of attaching spikes to her boots, and she made it nearly half-way up before they shot her down. Warden Kirov didn't kill her—she had them leave her on the ground for an entire day before they took her to the infirmary. Mila lost her hand; she limps and she has only one eye, Valor. One eye." Katia shakes her head. "They stuck her back in the cellblock after that as a warning to all of us. You've seen how punishment works here. If one person does some-thing wrong, they punish everyone. If you get caught trying to take people out of here, I don't know what they'd do."

Her words dry my mouth and try to melt my resolve like snow on skin.

"Just . . . think about it," I whisper. "Nobody ever did what I'm planning before. We're going *under*. Under the whole prison. There are tunnels that run underground from the prison to the city. One even goes to the palace. It's an old escape route for the royal family in case of trouble. My father had secret maps—"

Behind us, the door rattles. Our Peacekeeper opens it, and Peacekeeper Rurik enters.

"Valor, come with me," he says.

I jump to my feet, imagining all sorts of horrible things. Warden Kirov heard me somehow. Or she knows that I found Sasha last night. Or they saw me steal the sheet or the silver pick. I'm going to be searched and punished.

I snatch up my furs and throw them around myself, only then turning to Rurik, who waits in the doorway. I know better than to ask him where I'm being taken. He leads me out of the laundry and toward the tower. I look to the slit window again and draw in a breath. There's no one behind the glass, but someone is out on the battlements of the inner wall of the prison. It must be deep enough to have a walkway across the top of it.

The figure sees me and heads back toward the tower as Peacekeeper Rurik and I reach the rounded wooden door at the bottom. I go rigid. I would recognize that blue tunic, those gray furs, that face anywhere. And I should, because they belong to the boy I've been convicted of attempting to murder. I'm not being taken before Warden Kirov. I'm being taken before His Royal Highness Prince Anatol of Demidova.

In truth, I never expected to see him again. But this is also the first bit of luck I've yet had. The tunnel I plan to use can be accessed right beneath this very tower.

Peacekeeper Rurik pulls the heavy wooden door open, and I note the thick barrel of the lock as we enter. He closes and locks the door behind us.

Under my feet is a thick blue carpet, cut circular to fit the room. The tower could have been taken right from the palace itself. White marble, gold filigree, plush blue velvet drapes along the walls. Ahead of me is a spiral staircase going up through the tower. I take a deep breath to slow the pounding of my heart when I see that it also goes down. There's a room below this one, below ground level, and somewhere down there is the entrance to a tunnel that only I, out of the three hundred prisoners at Tyur'ma, know anything about.

"Up," says Peacekeeper Rurik, his deep voice filling the chamber. He follows me as I climb the polished staircase, curling up past a first floor with a number of finely carved chairs around a shining chestnut table, a second floor filled entirely with shelves full of books, a third with only a music stand and a violin, and finally to the highest part of the tower, a room with a cone-shaped roof and a dark wooden desk, a severe-looking Prince Anatol seated behind it.

Peacekeeper Rurik takes up a stance at the back of the room. Prince Anatol levels a steely look at him. "You may wait downstairs."

I'm surprised, then worried. He means to speak with me alone?

Peacekeeper Rurik seems to hesitate. I don't blame him. For all anyone else knows, he'd be leaving our future queen's brother alone with a vengeful would-be killer.

Prince Anatol gives him a haughty, expectant look, and Peacekeeper Rurik turns slowly and descends the stairs. I feel like I can hear his footsteps all the way to the bottom.

Prince Anatol waits until we're alone, leaving me standing in the middle of the room, before he speaks.

"You tried to kill me." It's somewhere between a statement and a question.

"It seems that way," I say.

He gets up and comes around to the front of the desk, which he leans against with his arms folded, his head tilted. "Either you did or you didn't."

"I did." I fight the rush of shame and look sullenly at the carpet. Perhaps that's all he wishes to hear.

"I would like to know why."

I look up at him then. His dark hair curls at the front despite someone's obvious effort to stop it from doing so. It's always done that. Once, I watched him during one of the long and boring ceremonies Sasha and I sometimes had to attend with our parents, and he spent half of the time trying to make the front of his hair lie straight. He's not that little boy anymore, though. And the link between our families is severed.

I lock my hands behind my back, standing the way Katia does at her cell door each morning. "Your Highness, I believe you know why."

"I would like to hear you say it." He watches me sharply.

I square my shoulders. I'm starting to sweat. "Revenge," I say. "Revenge on your family for putting my sister in prison for life." The anger I feel when I say this is real. It's even hotter and clearer than it was before, now that I know she's innocent. I blame myself for not believing that right from the start.

"Yes," he says shortly. "Your sister the thief."

I say nothing. Let him keep believing she did it; the time for trying to protest anyone's innocence is long gone. I can feel the bulk of the sheet wedged around my waist. If he orders me searched, if he even suspects I'm anything but a wicked prisoner, I'll be caught with a stolen sheet, soap, and in my boot a metal pick that could kill someone.

"Do you know why she did it?" he asks, standing straight and moving closer to me. "I assume you saw the trial. You know she wouldn't tell anyone where the music box was. Has she told you where it is?"

I keep my gaze fixed on the polished wood of the desk.

Prince Anatol stands in front of me. The golden fist clasping his cloak shines at his neck. "Your prince is speaking to you," he says. "Do you know anything about the music box? Answer."

I look him in the eye, hoping he can't see that I'm shaking. "I haven't seen my sister. I know nothing of why she stole the box or where she put it, Your Highness. Nothing at all." Maybe it's enough that I really have no idea where the music box is. I pray that it is.

Prince Anatol turns his head and stares up at the ceiling. "Your parents have tried to petition my mother at least three times already," he says. "Don't you care anything for them?"

"You know I do," I snap, much too loudly.

"Then tell me what I want to know."

"I . . . I can't. I don't know anything," I say, misery filling me up and making my throat tight. "Are they well? Are my parents well?"

The prince's mouth presses together. "They're as well as my own parents. You've betrayed us all. How do you think they feel?"

I shake my head. I can't speak.

"It would be better for you *and* your sister if you told the truth. I'm determined to find out one way or another."

Whatever he means by that, it makes me shiver. I know his reputation well enough to believe that he won't rest, like a hunting dog with the scent of prey in its nose.

"No answer for me?" he asks, his mouth still in that compressed line.

I say nothing.

"Then leave," he says. "But I'll see you again, Valor."

I take a small step back, then another, then I flee down the stairs as fast as I can. The violin, the books, the chairs blur past, and I'm breathless by the time I reach the bottom, where Peacekeeper Rurik waits. I barely see him. All I can think about is the prince. He's too interested, far too interested in the music box. Or maybe he's interested in who else knows that it wasn't my sister who stole it at all.

CHAPTER 9

The next day's evening meal sits in front of me on the long wooden table in the ice hall. It's some kind of potato and cabbage broth. I'm hungry, but I haven't touched it yet. Katia is steadily eating hers. The bluish ice blocks around us make it look as though she's underwater. She doesn't look at me, but Feliks, sitting opposite her, wants to know everything about my trip to the tower and Prince Anatol's questioning. Yesterday Peacekeeper Rurik hovered close after he returned me to the laundry, and I've had no chance to speak to Feliks since. Today we were rotated to work on maintaining the ice buildings with another group, and it was impossible to talk at all.

Katia is still sulking from watching me hide the things I stole in our cell. I put the sheet flat under my mattress, the soap inside a split seam, and the pick—well, I had no choice but to tie that to the underside of Katia's bedframe using ripped strips of material. I would have put it on mine, but it wouldn't have been hidden, and I can't carry everything I need to get Sasha out around with me. I lay awake for a long time after that, wanting to ask Katia what she was going to do now that she knew my plan, but at the same time not wanting to ask in case it tipped her over into telling Warden Kirov.

"What are we going to do next?" whispers Feliks. We've perfected the art of using the shadows from the torchlight in the hall to cover our faces and talking while barely moving our mouths. I bet we look ridiculous, but it works.

I lean forward over my bowl, lifting my spoon. "I have to borrow a bunch of keys," I say. "I already have soap to make impressions of them, and metal to melt down and make copies."

His eyes go big with excitement. I can't help but like the way he's hanging on my every word, even if Katia is still silent.

"How are you going to get the keys?"

I hesitate. I need to steal them, but I've never stolen anything before, not from an actual person.

"I thought you had this all planned," says Katia. She sounds a little bit smug, as though she's glad I'm confirming that I don't know what I'm doing.

"I do have a plan," I say, feeling defensive. "Once I get the keys, I can get out of the cell at night, get to the tower, and find the tunnel. Then . . . well, it's just a matter of timing."

"Easy," she says. "After you steal a bunch of keys from a Peacekeeper and get your sister away from the Black Hands."

I take a deep breath, and then another while I think of something to say. But really, I don't know how I'm going to do either of those things, and she's putting doubts in my head that I'll be able to pull them off.

"What's that noise?" says Feliks.

We stop eating, and I notice half the heads in the hall are turned toward the door. Outside, there are footsteps running across the snow, calls between Peacekeepers, and, faintly, in the background, the howls of wolves.

The door bursts open, and the Peacekeeper with the chessboard tattoos fills the space. He thrusts a torch into the room and shouts, "All Peacekeepers to the wall. Get the prisoners back to the cellblock now!"

There are two Peacekeepers in the hall with us. One runs from the back of the hall, and everyone watches him, soldered to their seats by the fear of standing and earning an infraction. He joins the one who came to issue the orders and they both hurry away, the torch a bobbing flare of light across the prison grounds. They're heading to the wall.

"Line up. Back to the cells now," shouts our remaining Peacekeeper above the shocked murmurs in the hall. We all stand, hustle into our usual lines, and follow him out into the cold night. Torches burn along the top of the inner wall, blotting out the darkness in a ring around the grounds.

Heads are twisted toward the wall as we walk, whispers passing along the line. Everyone is shuffling slower than usual despite the cold. Along the battlements, the shapes of Peacekeepers move. The length of a bow juts above the crenellated wall. Wolves bay and howl out on the plains. I know the sound. They're agitated. They're hunting. It raises the tiny hairs on the back of my neck, and I shiver.

I snag the coat of the person in front of me. "What's happening?"

It's Natalia. But right now, she's too interested in what's going on to ignore me. "I heard there's a prison cart on its way, and the wolves are trying to attack. They're saying Prince Anatol is out there."

My heart beats faster. That's what the Peacekeepers are doing—trying to protect the cart.

"I need to speak with Warden Kirov," I say.

Natalia's eyes widen. "You can't."

But I've already turned and lost my place in the line to go back to the Peacekeeper herding us into the cellblocks. Nicolai frowns as I pass him.

I'm out of breath when I reach the Peacekeeper, who's reaching for the pouch at his belt to issue me an infraction.

"Wait. Please. I need to speak to Warden Kirov. I want to offer my services to help."

"Prisoners need to return to the cellblocks," he says.

"I've been trained for this," I say, my pulse bounding. "If it's true that there's a cart out there and that I could have saved it and so could you, what do you think Warden Kirov will say if she finds out you stood in my way instead of using me?"

Then I see her, Warden Kirov herself, striding across the grounds toward the tower.

"Warden Kirov, I can help!" I call out.

She doesn't break stride, but this is my chance to get Sasha away from the Black Hands, I know it. I run toward the warden.

There's a shout from the Peacekeeper behind me. I run faster, my boots kicking up snow. A familiar whistling sound shoots past my ear, and an arrow hits the ground to my left. I flinch away, sliding on the ice underfoot. One of the Peacekeepers up on the wall reloads, his weapon pointed at me. "Halt!"

I skid to a stop, breath coming fast as a hunted fox. Boots crunch on the snow behind me, and my arms are grabbed on either side. It's Nicolai and another prisoner. "Peacekeeper says you'll pay for this," says Nicolai grimly. He widens his eyes like he's trying to tell me something. But I don't know what it is.

Just ahead, the warden has stopped. "Bring her," she calls.

Nicolai and the girl on my other side march me forward. We reach Warden Kirov at the bottom of the tower. "I might have known it would be you," she says, and nods to my two captors. "Take her back to the cells. You will have extra rations, and she will be punished later for her reckless disregard for people's lives when we need every woman and man on the wall."

I curl my hands into fists. I know it's more than pushing my luck to speak again, but I can't stop now.

"You have to let me help. You need me. I'm the best shot here, and if you put a bow in my hands, I promise you that Prince Anatol will pass through the gates without so much as a scratch on his royal person."

She barks a laugh. "Given the crime that put you here, I can hardly believe that. What does a promise from someone like you mean?"

I keep my voice level. "I'm already in prison. What would I gain from hurting the prince now? My sister, Sasha, is with the Black Hands. But if I saved the prince, you could let her out so I could see her sometimes. It's my sister's safety at stake. I have every reason to be honorable, and none to let you down."

The warden gives one sharp shake of her head. "Take her away."

"Warden!" The cry comes from the Peacekeeper who fired at me. "The wolves are closing in."

Nicolai and the girl pull me backward, and the warden hurries into the tower.

"Valor, stop it," says Nicolai in a low voice.

I barely hear him. "If he's going to die anyway, then you have nothing to lose! Give me a chance!" I yell.

She stops. I point to the Peacekeeper's arrow behind us in the snow. "They've already shown you how safe the prince is right now. I can do this."

I wait, holding my breath.

She leaves it a beat too long, and my hope melts like snow in summer.

Finally, she says, "Come."

I wrench my arms free and dart forward. Warden Kirov tracks snow up the winding staircase in the tower, and I add to it, rushing after her until we reach the room where Prince Anatol made me answer those questions. One of the dark wooden panels that make up the walls is open— a hidden doorway to the battlements. We sweep out onto the brightly lit walkway where the wind cuts through the notches in the crenellated walls.

There are six Peacekeepers standing at intervals along the wall, all armed with bows. Warden Kirov steps straight to the wall facing the plains. Her hands grip the rough stone, her face tight.

"Stop the wolves and allow that cart safe passage. If you cut so much as a button from his tunic, your sister will pay for it."

I step to a rack of longbows and a barrel full of arrows on one side of the walkway. A thrill flashes through me. I love to shoot. I think about the last time I let an arrow fly. I wanted to miss my target then as much as I want to hit it now.

I take a bow and feel the shape and balance of it in my hands. I've missed this.

Along the wall, the Peacekeepers take aim. The cart is far off in the snow, but I can see the black horses running flat out even at this distance. I count sixteen wolves loping in a loose formation, some beginning to draw level with the horses, though they're not yet close enough to attack.

A wolf lets out a bloodcurdling howl on the plain, and a Peacekeeper releases an arrow. It's too soon. He must not know how far an arrow will fly, and I can tell without looking that he won't hit his mark. His stance is wrong. There's a sharp breeze blowing, and I doubt he's taken that into account.

"They're trying to surround the cart," says the Peacekeeper next to me. He draws back his bow. I was right about the shot already taken. The dark dart of an arrow lies out on the snow.

I step behind him and take a look down the sights. "They'll take the horses down first."

He looks over his shoulder. "How do you know that?"

"I know about all the animals in the realm," I say, then wish I hadn't. I don't want to talk about who I am or why I'm here.

"Bring them down!" The warden's voice rings out over the wall.

Howls come from all over now. There's more than one pack out there, watching. Their calls are wild, raising goose bumps all over my body. The cart seemed so solid when I rode in it, so final. Now it looks small and breakable, like one of Sasha's old clockwork toys.

The Peacekeeper readies himself to shoot. I see the wolf he intends to hit, running at the front of the pack. Sleek and black, ruffed with white fur, almost as big as the horses. It's gaining ground, snow flying in its wake.

I lean over and adjust his aim slightly. His shot would have been close, but mine will hit. "Trust me," I say. He looks to Warden Kirov, and she nods. The arrow whistles through the air and the wolf drops, plowing a furrow through the snow.

One of the other Peacekeepers must have hit too, because another animal farther down the pack twists in the air, then falls and starts dragging itself along the ground.

I open my mouth to say "Finish it," but the Peacekeeper has already reloaded and let his arrow fly. The wolf slackens like a puppet with its strings cut, but the other animals haven't slowed. Their bodies are sleek and strong, muscles rippling as they run. One of them nears the blindered horse on the right. Its paws pound the ground, throwing up sprays of snow. A snarl rips from its mouth as its jaws open to attack. The horse rears, whinnying in terror, its flanks shining with sweat against the snowy backdrop.

A barrage of arrows fly out, but everyone is too scared of hitting the horse, not willing to be the one who brings down the cart instead, and the wrath of Warden Kirov with it.

The cart is close enough now that I can see a much smaller figure seated next to the man who brought me here. It's true, then. The figure clinging to the cart, unprotected as it thunders toward the prison, is Prince Anatol. Warden Kirov stares intently at the scene, still gripping the wall.

Two more wolves are down, but the rest are still hunting; twelve, maybe thirteen of them are left. They must be desperate.

I load my bow, the weight of it in my hands so familiar it's like an extension of my arm. My body goes still as I take aim, factor in the wind, judge the distance. I breathe out and release my first arrow, relishing the feel of the bow in my hands. A wolf goes down. Swift as a hare, I fire another, and another. The animals fall, and my focus never wavers.

The wolf running by the horse has dropped back slightly. I think it's tiring, but then I see the direction of its gaze.

My blood freezes. Peacekeeper Rurik is the new target. It's worked out that if he falls, the whole cart does.

"Valor!" Warden Kirov sees it too, sees the bloodbath that we'll be watching if one of us doesn't hit that wolf.

It has to be me.

I take aim. I watch. I breathe. I wait. I wait.

I fire.

The arrow wings the wolf, catching his shoulder and spinning him around. I reload faster than anyone has ever reloaded and shoot again, and again. Every arrow hits its mark.

Darkness seeps into the snow around the still body of the wolf.

The cart comes thundering into the last stretch with still more wolves chasing it, and I hear the gate opening far below. The prisoners' terrified faces are upturned to us, staring through the bars of the cage on the cart. One of them steadies herself, her cuffed hands wrapped around the bars above her head. She looks straight at me, eyes wide, face pinched with fear.

My hands move, fluid as dancers, taking aim, feeling the cutting wind. There's only me and the cart and the wolves stopping me from getting the one thing I want most of all—Sasha next to me. I shoot and shoot, again and again, until the cart disappears underneath us with a scraping noise, whinnying from the horses, and cries from the prisoners in the cart.

I stop. The snow below is littered with the lifeless bodies of wolves. Dark stains mat their fur and blot the snow. I bow my head for a second, and when I turn, Warden Kirov is stock-still, staring at me. The Peacekeepers circle her, and everyone is looking at me.

"I told you, I . . . have some skill with a bow," I say.

CHAPTER 10

A smile starts to creep across my face, my heart soaring. I saved Prince Anatol, and though nobody may know it, I can hold my head up again. Best of all, I've gotten what I needed, and in the most unexpected way. I think Sasha will like Feliks, and he will like her. Even Katia won't be able to resist once she meets my sister.

Warden Kirov sweeps toward me. "I must meet with the prince. A Peacekeeper will return you to your meal." Crisis over, she's returned to her calm, cold self.

I hold in the grin that's trying to burst out of me as I return my weapon to the stand.

Warden Kirov stares at me, her head tilted. "I did the right thing letting you do that."

"I'm very happy I could help."

"Yes. I'm sure you are. The young prince takes a great interest in the workings of the prison of late. He decided to ride with Peacekeeper Rurik out of curiosity, ahead of the royal visit tomorrow."

I say nothing, but she must see my surprise. "Oh, yes, Valor—while the search for the music box continues, the royal family and Lady Olegevna are touring Demidova. The prince will of course be heavily guarded tonight, as will the rest of the family tomorrow."

She gestures, and we start walking toward the tower and into the topmost room and down the spiral staircase behind the Peacekeepers.

"Warden Kirov, about my sister, Sasha. When can she—"

"Ah, yes." The warden smiles pleasantly. "That was a most impressive display tonight, Valor. Truly astounding. With regards to introducing your sister into the general population, regrettably, this will not be possible; but on behalf of His Royal Highness, we thank you for your service."

Warden Kirov walks away, and I stand speechless on the thick, blue carpet on the ground floor of the tower. She promised. My face gets hot. I clench my fists to stop myself from breaking something.

"Move," says the Peacekeeper. I barely look at him as I follow the order, leaving the tower and walking back to the ice hall. Its eerie blue sheen rises up from the snow, still lit from within by torchlight.

Inside, Nicolai and the girl who held my arms are eating. There's a bowl waiting for me. There's a big hunk of bread too. I should be as happy as Nicolai looks to get extra rations, but all I can think about is Warden Kirov.

The Peacekeeper deposits me next to Nicolai and moves into the corner. On the other side of the room, there's another small group of prisoners. One of them, a broad girl with rough, unbraided hair, shifts quickly into another seat, and through the gap, I see a face beaming at me. Sasha. We're here so late that the Black Hands are having their meal. There are two Peacekeepers with them, one standing in each corner.

I keep my head down, but as I lift my spoon, I wave. It's so good to see her that I regain my lost appetite and begin spooning the lukewarm potato broth into my mouth.

"I'm sorry about chasing after you and holding you back from the warden like that. I had no choice," murmurs Nicolai. He almost looks anxious that I believe him, as if he feels bad.

I shrug and turn my attention back to Sasha. I suppose this is how he gains his responsibilities in the mines, by doing as he's told. I'd be angrier with him but for the fact I can see my sister.

"Who is that girl over there grinning at us like a lunatic?" he asks.

"That's—" I hesitate, but there's no harm in telling him. "It's my sister."

Nicolai takes a good look at Sasha. "She looks like you."

I open my mouth and then close it. We're not identical. Sasha has big dark-brown eyes, bronze skin a shade darker than mine, and glossy, braided hair. Her features are even and pleasing, and when she smiles, her face sparkles. She is beautiful, and I have never thought she looked like me.

The Black Hands sitting around her dwarf her, and my heart cracks to think I tried my best and still couldn't get her away from them. As I watch, trying to tell her how sorry I am with my eyes, she picks up her spoon and jams the handle into her hunk of bread. Then she reaches across and takes the spoon of the girl next to her. I almost push to my feet in horror, but the girl just sits there as my sister does the same thing to the girl's bread, holds the two spoons in front of her, and makes the bread walk down the table.

Despite everything, I feel a sense of wonder and a smile building inside me. Father used to do this at dinnertime to make us laugh. And if he came home from work frowning, we'd do it for him, each of us responsible for one of the bread feet.

She's charmed the Black Hands in some way, like she does everyone else. And if she can do that, if she can smile after everything that's happened to her, just to cheer me up, then I can carry on too. I will get her out of here, no matter what Warden Kirov does. The two tall Black Hands on either side of Sasha block the Peacekeepers' view of her, and when she pulls a funny face and makes the bread dance, I let my smile out.

~ ⌒∽ᘒᥳ⌒ ~

The cellblock is silent when we're taken back after the meal. Katia is asleep facing the wall as the Peacekeeper opens the cell door. I try not to stare too long at the bunch of keys attached to his belt. The bowl of water sits in its usual place at the back of the cell. I look at Katia, then sigh and plunge my hands into it, scrubbing quickly. I duck down to the floor and check that the pick is secure, flat against the slats on Katia's bed, and then I climb up to my bunk.

Lying in my bed, I stare at the wall with the blanket drawn up over my shoulder. The soap hidden in my mattress digs into my side, and I shuffle forward.

"What happened?" asks Katia quietly.

I hold still for a moment, surprised that she's talking to me. But she asked, and I want to tell someone. I tell her about Prince Anatol and the wolves and Warden Kirov. And even though seeing Sasha afterward made me feel better, now it isn't enough. Wanting really badly to get her out of here isn't going to make it happen. I have to *do* it. And I thought I'd found the perfect way tonight. It isn't fair.

"I wish I'd shot him the first time," I say savagely, though it's Warden Kirov I'm actually furious with.

"The prince? What do you mean?"

I can't believe she's talking after we're in our bunks, much less that she wants to hear this now, but I tell her the whole story, right from the start—my plan to rescue Sasha, the parade where I shot at the prince, my arrest, and the way I stopped Feliks from escaping. All of it comes out in a whisper to the wall, until I've told her how Sasha didn't steal the music box and how we think her being kept in isolation has something to do with whoever did take it.

There's only quiet from the bunk below. I curl up tighter, pulling my knees to my chest. Maybe she's not interested. Maybe she fell asleep. She doesn't care that Sasha's innocent. I bite my lip. I didn't even believe it myself. Maybe I shouldn't have spilled everything out the way I did.

"Valor—who do you think took the box, then? And why was the prince asking you about it?"

So she *was* listening when I told Feliks about my little interrogation. My head aches. I can think about the answers to those questions all day, but I'm not going to find out the truth stuck in here staring at a wall.

I sigh. "I don't know. He must think I know something, or that Sasha does." Something new occurs to me; maybe it's what Katia was trying to say. "And if he had something to do with it himself and thinks we know about it . . ."

Her voice comes back after a while, just as I'm thinking it all through. She's thinking the exact same thing I am. "You have to get out of here soon."

"Yes," I say, thinking of Sasha, alone up in her cell.

"*We* have to get out of here soon."

The words are so quiet I think they might only have been in my head. "What did you—?"

"I'm going to help you."

"Why?" It slips out before I can stop it. She's been so certain that none of my plans can work. And after today, I was beginning to believe her.

"Why do you need to know that?" Now she sounds peevish again. "Isn't it enough that I'm in?"

It is. So I say nothing.

"Valor?"

"Yes?"

There's a long pause. "Thanks for washing your hands."

As we rush out of the cellblock in the morning toward the ice hall and breakfast, I look to the tower. I don't know what I expect to see, but there's nothing out of place, nothing to suggest the prince is inside. I don't see Feliks either, though I look for him after the hectic spill from the cells is over and we've gotten our bowls of food.

Once we've eaten and are standing behind our stools waiting for our orders, Warden Kirov steps into the ice hall. Everyone stands straighter. I clench my jaw, unwilling to even look at her.

"We are expecting to be graced with a royal inspection today as part of the tour of the realm Queen Ana and Lady Olegevna are conducting," she says. "As such, there will be dire consequences for anyone exhibiting any . . . infraction-worthy behavior. There may also be chances to earn rewards." She smiles but doesn't elaborate. I seethe, knowing that she doesn't mean it at all.

She summons Nicolai and speaks with him quietly for a moment. While she's talking, she glances at me. It sends a flash of anger through me, followed by fear. I hate feeling so helpless.

Nicolai assumes his position at the head of the room, just as he does every morning. Warden Kirov leaves without looking at me again, and Nicolai starts to hand out work detail. I'm relieved when he announces our group will be in the mines today. No one likes the work, but I was expecting something worse.

As we separate, Nicolai smiles, so fast that I think maybe I imagine it, but when he moves back to lead us to the mine, Feliks is standing behind him, and I remember why I need to talk to him. I fall in line between Feliks and Katia. "There's something I need to ask you later," I whisper to him.

I'm the first to light my torch, tools in hand, ready to disappear down whatever tunnel Nicolai tells me to. The faster we get to the mine, the faster we can be rid of our Peacekeeper escort and I can speak with Feliks. But it seems Nicolai has other ideas.

"Natalia, you're in charge today. Take these four and work the malachite shaft. Can I trust you?"

Natalia nods. I look at Feliks and he looks at me, understanding that we can't speak freely in front of Nicolai.

With our torches raised, we split from Natalia's group and take a tunnel on the far right. It's pitch-black and narrow, and my heart sinks. I'm impatient to tell Feliks my plan. And now, though he's right behind me, close enough for me to touch, I may have to go all day without getting a chance.

A soft glow of light warms the space ahead of me. Nicolai and Katia pass through the tunnel into a cave, and I follow. Stunning swirls of pink minerals are studded through the white rock of the mountain, but it's the glow surrounding us that makes me stare in wonder. Up on the high roof there are hundreds of points of light, glowing like the night sky has been caught in a net and cast into this cavern.

"Valor?" Nicolai has holstered his torch in a bracket on the wall. "Can I speak to you about something? Katia, you can be in charge until I get back." His eyes flit between us, and he shifts from one foot to the other.

Katia and I exchange a glance. I don't know what's going on, but I can hardly say no. My chest tightens as I follow Nicolai away from the others.

"Let's go this way." Nicolai walks right by me, using the light from the torch I'm holding; it's the only one we have now. He leads the way into a narrow shaft that twists up and seems to fold back the way we came, toward the surface. It's cold and airless, blacker than night outside the glow of the torch.

"Where are we going?" I ask, my voice loud and sounding far more scared than I wanted it to. I'm ready to bash him on the head with my torch and run if I have to, but without Sasha there would be no point.

He stops in the tiny space. I hold my torch out to the side, away from our bodies. His face is lit from one side. My heart pounds hard. There's light coming from ahead of us, but I might be mistaken.

"Valor, there *is* something I wanted to— What's the matter?" He looks concerned. I can't work him out.

"Nothing," I say. "What do you want to speak to me about?" I sound gruff and suspicious.

"Warden Kirov asked me today to keep you out of sight during the royal visit. I couldn't ask her why, but I thought . . . I thought I could ask you."

I frown. What does she think I'm going to do? Hurl snow at them in retribution? The more I think about it, though, the more I want to see them. Without them seeing me. I'm not going to get another chance after today, and someone wants me out of the way for this visit. Maybe the same someone who framed Sasha.

"There are lots of ledges and fissures in these mountains, aren't there?" I ask. "Places we could watch the royal visiting party from?"

"What?" Nicolai stops. He frowns, and then understanding flashes across his face. "I don't think that's a good idea."

"You wanted to talk to me, didn't you? If you know somewhere we can go to see the royal family, we can talk there. Okay?"

Nicolai bites his lip. "There's something going on, isn't there? You're planning to—"

He stops dead. Suddenly, I think we're on the same page. I think we both have the word "escape" in our heads. But I'm not going to be the one to say it. He may have been nice to me, but he has the ear of the warden far too often for me to blurt out my plans now.

I stare at him.

He looks around us, sighs, and then starts walking. After a while he says, sounding a bit sullen, "Okay. Just ahead there's an opening in the cliff. Be careful, though."

Ice-blue sky shows through the crack in the rock.

"You have it all wrong, you know," he says. "You can trust me. I only wanted to talk to you alone to be careful.

There; I've done what you wanted. Now tell me. You have a plan, don't you?"

I place my feet carefully and walk to the edge of the fissure in the cliff. It opens onto sky and a sheer drop down to the ground. We're a little higher than the walls surrounding Tyur'ma. I pull back a step, breathing the clear, cold mountain air.

"I don't know what you mean," I say.

Nicolai stands on the other side of the gap. "Listen, it might not seem like it, but I was trying to help you last night by the tower. I saw today that Warden Kirov didn't do as she said she would and let your sister in with the rest of us." He gazes out over the prison. "I could have told you she wouldn't keep her word."

I shrug and say nothing. She doesn't seem to have a problem keeping her word to Nicolai.

"I have eyes, Valor—and a working brain. I see you with Katia and Feliks. I hear things about why your sister is in here, and why you are. I know this all has something to do with the prince, I know you're planning something, and do you know what else I know? That I want in on it. Just . . . think about it, okay?"

In the distance, the onion domes of the palace are bright, reaching up above the spread of the city. The houses and businesses, the docks, the school, the cobbled square, and the golden gates around the palace gardens—it's all so beautiful. And so far removed from where we stand.

I can't help but think about what Nicolai's asking me, but that doesn't mean I'm going to answer him.

"I didn't think you could miss a place," I say. But I do. Deep in my chest, I miss home. Miss the four of us being together, being happy. Will I ever be able to go into the city again? Or will I only ever see it like this, from afar?

I pretend I can see my house—the one that doesn't belong to us anymore—where I used to live with Mother and Father and Sasha. Pretend I can see the target in the garden that Mother made for me to practice shooting when I was little. A few months ago I climbed onto our roof and hit it from there, remembering when it towered above me and my arrows used to fly wide and miss it altogether.

"Do you miss your family?" I ask. "Do you have one?"

His face softens. "Of course I do. I don't want to be here any more than you do. If I had a choice—" He cuts himself off as though he's said too much, then looks at the floor. "You and your sister are going to escape," he says quietly. "You don't have to admit it. But I've already helped you, and you know it. I could have told the warden you weren't paying attention right from the first time we worked the mines. But I didn't. You can tell me what you're planning if you want. That's all I wanted to say. You can't hold it against me that I act like a model prisoner so I can make the warden like me."

As he stops talking, there's movement below. Out from the tower, onto the battlements, a procession of people appears. Warden Kirov comes first at a brisk walk, followed by Lady Olegevna. Her headdress of pearls glows milky white, and her deep purple cloak sweeps the floor behind her as she walks.

We duck into a crouch in the shadows on my side of the opening. I pass the torch back to Nicolai, and he holds it low to the ground.

The queen herself, dazzling in white, steps out. The king follows. In the prison grounds, those who are working on the ice buildings openly stare until a Peacekeeper shouts for them to keep working.

The warden gestures, and her voice carries faintly on the wind. The queen nods, her eyes made up with a mask of black filigree. Her braids spill in loops and twists from under her *ushanka*.

Prince Anatol and his sister, Princess Anastasia, walk out side by side, their heads close together. I motion Nicolai to get back, and then lean into the shadows in our narrow hiding place. The royal siblings stand a little apart from their mother, gazing out over the prison. Prince Anatol looks none the worse for his second brush with death in as many weeks. His hair, ruffled by the breeze, curls at the front, and the gold on his tunic and cloak shines in the morning sun. Next to him, his sister's white-gloved hands are clasped in front of her. Her eyes are painted in a simple, striking design, black under the snow-white fur of her *ushanka*.

But by far the most riveting things about them both are the harsh, straight lines of their mouths and the rigid poses of their bodies. The prince brings his hands up, and then seems to remember himself and forces them down again.

I glance back at Nicolai. He's frowning. He shakes his head, telling me he doesn't know why it's happening any more than I do, but we see the same thing—the prince and the princess are having a blazing fight.

CHAPTER 11

Nicolai and I watch the prince and princess fight. Anatol's fists are clenched at his sides, his brows pulled low over his eyes. His sister's mouth twists as she spits words at him. After a minute or two, the whole procession begins to move closer to us. Princess Anastasia storms off under the pretense of joining Warden Kirov at the front.

Then I realize it was no pretense. The princess is talking to the warden now, her features animated. She no longer seems angry, but she still tosses her head and glances at Anatol. The warden has her hands behind her back, her face unreadable as she walks. Anastasia leans in closer to the warden and points straight above the girls' cellblock. No, at the top of it, maybe. Warden Kirov's gaze fixes on the building, and then she bows to the princess just before they both disappear from view along the wall.

Silently, we slip back down the tunnel, Nicolai raising the torch as we descend into the mountain.

"What do you think that was about?" he asks.

"I have no idea," I say. "Though I'd dearly love to know."

"Didn't your sister used to work for the princess?"

"How do you know that?" I ask in a sharp voice.

"I just— I heard that she did."

The tunnel dips and twists around a corner. I put my hand to the wall to steady myself.

"Just how much else have you heard?" I'm annoyed that everyone seems to know my family's business.

His eyes are wide. "Nothing much," he says. "Only that she stole a music box from the palace."

"Well, then you heard wrong." I can't work out what's going on with the prince and the princess, only that something is. "My sister didn't steal anything. Someone else did and made sure she was blamed for it." The words come out angrier than I mean them to. I know it's not fair to Nicolai. It's my own guilt for believing my sister to be a thief that's talking, not real annoyance at him. But that only makes it worse.

He stops walking, and I can't go any farther now that he's carrying the torch.

"What?" I say shortly.

"Are you sure she didn't steal it? What—what are you going to do?"

I don't blink. I look straight at him. "What could I possibly do about it? Forget I said anything."

He hesitates, but then carries on walking. "Valor?" he says.

"What now?"

"We'll be working in the kitchens tomorrow."

"Why are you telling me that?"

He shrugs. "It might be useful information. Like I said, I want to help. I don't want to spend my life in here anymore than you do."

We walk on in silence until we get back to the glowing cave, where I find Katia and Feliks working away, talking as though they've known each other forever. It never ceases to amaze me how other people can do that. I watch Nicolai as he joins them under the soft, starry light. Maybe I can trust him after all. But I still decide to wait until our evening meal before I talk to Feliks.

The line for food snakes along the wall of the ice hall. I managed to get myself into a position with Feliks in front of me and Katia behind. Nicolai is farther forward, almost at the counter. Cold radiates from the translucent blocks of ice. I check for Peacekeepers and then lean forward to Feliks.

"It's time to get the keys. But I need your help."

He flashes a quick grin over his shoulder.

The line moves along, and I check around us again. "I have everything ready for when we have them. Can you do it?"

"I'm offended," he says. "I'm the best goods liberator in the city. Or at least I will be when I get out of here. If I get the keys, then I get to come with you. Deal?"

He gets to the front of the line and takes his bowl.

"Deal," I whisper, moving into position to get my food. The man with the wolves tattooed up his arms hands me a portion of watery soup and a hunk of bread. I turn around and almost pour the contents of my bowl straight onto the floor.

"Hello, Valor," says Sasha quietly. Her eyes are dancing, and she's bouncing on her toes. I can tell she wants to fling her arms around me. I want to do the same.

Instead, I steady my bowl and glance around for Peace-keepers. "What are you doing here?"

She grins, full of glee. "Well, I'm out, of course. You didn't expect me so soon?"

I can't believe it. It seems as though Peacekeepers should rush in and drag her away, like there's been a mis-take. I stand, dumbfounded, while she gets a bowl ahead of Katia. Then she takes my arm and tows me back down the room.

"How did you do it?" she asks. "What did you say?"

"What?" I shake my head. "I haven't done anything. I tried, but Warden Kirov lied to me—"

Sasha frowns. "No, not her. The queen."

I'm so lost. I can't believe she's here, holding onto my arm, but I can't focus on it properly until I understand what's happened.

"Sasha, stop. I didn't do this at all. I had nothing to do with getting you out. So start at the beginning. And whisper." We shuffle in between the tables, moving as slowly as possible. There are prisoners everywhere, waiting for their food or taking it to the tables. I have to stop myself from putting my arm around Sasha; we can't look as though we're talking.

"I was in the laundry with the Black Hands when Warden Kirov summoned me to the tower. Have you been in there? It's like the palace, Valor. There's this blue carpet, and—"

"Sasha."

"Okay, okay. She said I was to be released into the general population of the prison and that I'd have a cellmate on the block like everyone else from now on."

"That's it? She didn't say why?"

"She said, 'It seems that you have inspired royal mercy.' I thought you'd begged the queen and she'd ordered the warden to let me out."

I step in front of her, taking the lead so I can guide her to our table. "I had nothing to do with it," I say, heartily wishing that I had. It's starting to make sense nonetheless. "But I don't think it was the queen either." I tell her what I saw earlier on the wall—the princess talking to the warden, pointing to the part of the cellblock where the Black Hands are kept. I tell her about the princess and the prince arguing too.

Sasha's smile fades as we take our seats. "He's determined to keep me hidden so that nobody finds out I didn't take the music box, isn't he? Do you think he could have me put with the Black Hands again, Valor? I don't want to go back to the cell on my own."

I take her hand under the table and squeeze it. "Think, Sasha. You know the princess is far more powerful than Prince Anatol. She's the one who will inherit the throne. She's the one about to enter her thirteenth year now. He can't overrule anything she does. Even in here. Warden Kirov knows that. Don't worry."

I say it to comfort her. It's true that Anastasia will be queen, true that she has far more influence, but Anatol looked so angry on the wall today. So determined. He's always been the kind of boy who finds a way to get what he wants. We have to run. And we have to do it soon.

Sasha nods. "You're right. Maybe Anastasia's trying to help us. She thinks very deeply of late about the issues her mother faces now. Only a few months ago she questioned why Queen Ana was so set on an alliance with Magadanskya and not Pyots'k when Pyots'k could make us so much richer. Of course we all knew, and the queen and I explained to her why we must both put an end to the cold war with Maga-danskya and ignore the promise of riches from Pyots'k because of their intention to use our ports to launch their warships.

"Once we made her understand, she spent a lot of time thinking about the intricacies of alliances. Maybe she'll apply the same wisdom to the justice system, and to our predicament here." My sister's face has filled up with hope while she's been whispering, and that's more important to me than whatever politics she's talking about. It's won-derful to see her, to hear her chattering on about the same ideas she always used to talk about at home. Even if it does hurt to hear her still so enamored with the queen who put her here.

"Valor?" whispers Feliks as he sits down. On my other side, Katia joins us. All at once the joy of it hits me. Ever since I came here and found that Sasha was locked away, I've been missing part of my heart—a part I thought I'd have back when I got to Tyur'ma. Whatever else I lost by getting myself arrested, I thought that at least we'd be together. Then I arrived, and it's all been so hard, gone so wrong. Until now.

"Feliks, Katia—this is Sasha," I say, and before I know it my voice has cracked and I'm trying to hide the big tears

that roll down my cheeks. I don't let go of her hand. I cover
it with my own and wish that I could close my eyes and
transport us out of here and back to when we sat before the
fire at home, waiting for Mother and Father. I would give
anything.

Sasha's fingers twine into my own. "I'm all right, Valor.
And now we're together. It will be all right."

"We're all in it together," says Feliks.

"So," says Katia. She watches the Peacekeeper in the
corner as she murmurs the words. "There's really nothing
stopping us from getting out of here, is there?"

I look around at our group and nod. I think she's right.
I think it's time.

On the way back to the cellblock, I walk with my sister
ahead of me, and when we're inside, I watch to see which
cell they send her to. It's opposite mine and up one level.
Before we're ordered to step inside, I catch her eye, and she
lifts her hand, just at the wrist, and waves.

Maybe we could leave Demidova altogether, go to Magadanskya or somewhere beyond—somewhere Prince Anatol
won't find us. Maybe we can get word to Mother and Father
and all of us could go. We could take a ship from the docks,
find passage to another part of the world where music boxes
and royal families don't matter.

I step into the cell with Katia, and the bars blur in front
of me as the door rolls closed. I wipe my cheeks, barely

even hearing the noise the mechanism makes. After the roof groans and rumbles its way into place and the block is silent, I creep out of my bunk. Katia watches me as I remove the soap I stole from its hiding place inside one of the split seams of my mattress. Tomorrow, Nicolai had said, we will be working in the kitchens. I have my sister; now all I need are the keys.

"Nicolai got a message to me as we were walking back here," whispers Katia. She grins, and I wait expectantly. I don't think I've ever seen her smile like this before. It crinkles her eyes and warms her whole face.

"He's requested Sasha on our work detail tomorrow."

"Really?" My insides tingle and fizz. Everything is finally coming together. I don't think I'll sleep at all tonight.

"I think you could trust him, you know. If you wanted to."

Maybe I could. I tuck the soap securely into the wide brim of my hat and tie the earflaps up to hide it. The metal we're going to melt down to make copies of the keys will go into the secret compartment in my boot. I creep to the bars of our cell. The block is silent. A few dim torches flicker in brackets along the walls. I stare at the shadows, trying to make out Sasha's cell. I can't believe that I once protested at having to share a room with her when our parents had guests staying at the house. My heart reaches out over the gap between us now, wishing she were in this cell with me.

I crouch and reach for the silver pick strapped to the slats under Katia's bunk.

I reach farther, my fingers groping in the dark.

"What are you doing?" asks Katia.

"I can't reach it. Let me just—" I flip onto my back, the cold from the floor seeping into my furs as I wriggle under the bed. I feel all over the slats, then push myself farther under. My fingers grasp the thin strips of torn material I used to bind the pick to the bedframe. The edges are sliced. The bindings have been cut. My pick is gone.

CHAPTER 12

I yank myself out from under the bed and scramble up to face Katia. "Where is it?"

Katia swings her legs over the edge of her bed and sits up. "The pick? The pick's gone?" There's panic in her voice.

"What else would I be talking about?" I push my hands through my hair, fingers catching on my braids.

"Well, why are you asking me?"

"Who else would I ask?" I hiss at her.

She pulls her knees up to her chest. "I don't know where it is any more than you do. Someone's been in here, Valor." She looks around as if she expects them to still be here, or that there'll be some big clue to who it was.

I don't know what to think. I only know I should never have trusted anyone but me. "Why did you change your mind about helping me?" I start to pace the cell. Four steps by four, back and forth. "All you could talk about was how dangerous it was, how it couldn't be done, and then suddenly you wanted to come with us. Why is that?"

She gets up off the bed, and I'm reminded that she's taller than me. "It wasn't me, Valor. If I wanted to stop you, I could have told Warden Kirov days ago."

"Then why the change of heart?" I demand. We're both keeping our voices down, but there's so much fire in what I say. If she's been working against me the whole time . . .

Katia takes a step forward. "You're not thinking straight." She brings up her hand in the time that I blink, then flicks me right on the forehead.

We both stand there for a second, shocked, and then I let out a brief laugh before stifling it with my hand. It's just such a ridiculous thing for her to do. She smiles.

"I'm sorry," I say. "You're right. It makes no sense that you would have told Warden Kirov. We wouldn't be in here unpunished if she knew, would we?"

Katia drops back onto her bunk.

I join her on the bed, and we both stare at the flickering shadows on the wall for a while. Does someone know about my plans? Are they toying with me?

"You asked me why I want to help you." Katia's voice wrenches me from the maze I'm tangled in. She keeps looking at the wall, and I can just make out the freckles across her cheek. "Do you remember what you were talking about the night I agreed to help?"

I think back. I've been here such a short amount of time, but so much has happened. "I told you the whole story," I say. "Is that what changed your mind?"

She looks at her hands clasped in her lap. "It was the way you talked about Sasha. It was how much you needed to get her out of here. How much you'd given up to try something that is, frankly, impossible. I—" Her jaw tightens, and when she lifts her head, her eyes are shining. She swipes a hand over them. "I had a sister, once. We were close, like you and Sasha. But she was younger than me. I should have stayed at home to look after her; my mother asked me to, but I didn't. When I got back—saints, all I had wanted to do was go to a silly festival—she was gone. She'd drowned. It's my fault that she died. And then everything that I did afterward—running away, stealing . . . that's why I'm here." Katia turns to me and her eyes are wet with tears, but they're bright and hopeful too. "But I can help you save your sister. And maybe if I do . . . maybe if I do the right thing now—" She takes a ragged breath. "Sasha didn't even steal the music box. She's innocent, and she doesn't deserve to be here."

I put my arm around her. "I'm sorry, Katia," I whisper. "Thank you for helping. I don't think you deserve to be here either."

She makes a soft, bitter noise, so I pull her in tighter. I know what she's risking for me. "I'm not as good a sister as you think I am. I thought Sasha had stolen the box," I say. Saying the words makes me feel a little bit lighter.

Katia nods slowly. "But you came to save her anyway. That's what's important."

I feel even lighter. "Do you still think what we're trying to do is impossible?"

She looks up, the outline of her hair in silhouette. "Yes. But I know you're going to try all the same."

The kitchens are behind the ice hall, built with solid stone like the laundry, but only one story high. Huge chimneys rise from the roof, sending smoke into the light-blue sky. Feliks and Sasha walk beside me, both quiet since Katia and I told them about discovering the pick had disappeared last night. I put my hand on Sasha's shoulder the way I used to when we were little, just to reassure myself that she's really here. I feel unsettled and watchful with the other prisoners in our group, as if someone's watching me from the tower all the time, even though when I look there's no one there.

We pass a group headed for the mines. A downcast boy dragging his boots through the snow has a stripe of ink down his forehead. He's walking at a little distance from the others. The rest of the boys in the group look grim. It makes me sad that I know why.

The Peacekeeper with the chessboard tattoos stops at the kitchen doors, takes his keys from his belt, and unlocks the doors, leading us inside. Feliks elbows me in the ribs at the sight of the keys, hard enough for me to feel it through my layers of clothes.

Inside is one long, wide room. An enormous fireplace spans the length of the left-hand side. Over it there are spits and huge, blackened cooking pots. Two pitted wooden tables run down the other side of the room, and underneath them are drawers and cupboards. Pots and pans, grills and racks hang from the ceiling on chains.

"We need to light the fires, fill the pots with water to boil, and deal with that," Katia says, pointing to a huge pile of potatoes, carrots, and cabbages in sacks resting against the far wall. The earthy smell of them fills the room, mixed with a tinge of the breakfast porridge and something herbaceous. I spot tied bundles of dill and tarragon hanging from the ceiling.

"Sasha and I will light the fires," I say.

Natalia huffs. "Since when does she get to choose which jobs she gets?"

The Peacekeeper steps in, pointing at Natalia. "You will light the fires. The rest of you will fill the pots with water, peel the potatoes, and start washing." Beyond the fireplace at the back of the room is an alcove filled with sinks. Outside it, breakfast bowls for every inmate stand in stacks on the floor.

Feliks and I head for the sacks of vegetables. Big metal pans rest on the tables, and there are a handful of dull and blunted paring knives next to them. On the other side of the room, Natalia gathers bags of coal. Feliks watches them, his bright eyes missing nothing.

It seems like a lifetime ago that I ran over the rooftops with the guard chasing me, my heart beating out of my chest, forever since I met Feliks under that market stall with his bag full of stolen food.

I grab a potato, the first of what looks like thousands, and start to peel. "Do you know a lot of other people like you in the city?"

"People like what?"

I open my mouth to backtrack, apologize. I still sometimes sound like the girl whose mother works for the queen.

Feliks grins and shrugs, though. "It's sort of a network, you could say. Always useful to know where you can sell goods, who's in need of certain items, where it's safe to go, where the guards are going to be. We share information."

I drop a potato into a pan. "Before you got arrested for these *alleged* crimes, did you hear anything at all about the music box?"

Feliks considers. "There was plenty of talk about it when it went missing. But I imagine you soon took care of that."

I shake my head, not understanding him.

"Well, Valor, I don't know much about politics, but your sister *was* convicted of stealing it. And if you remember, you *did* try to kill a member of the royal family in the town square in front of everyone who's anyone, and a great deal of people who are nobody at all besides. I missed out on the gossip, what with getting arrested, but I think after that everyone might have been a *bit* distracted—" He stops talking and bites his lip. "Sorry. You don't want to hear that."

I don't. And yet I knew what people would say about my family after I did what I did. I knew, but I didn't want to think about it. The small mound of potatoes in the pan grows, and I drop a wet curl of peel to the floor. "But nothing in particular about the music box before we were arrested, though? No mention of it on the black market?"

Feliks shakes his head. I notice that he has yet to pick up a single potato. "I didn't pay much attention. But you're right—I didn't hear anything about it being sold." He frowns. "No rumor at all. And now that you bring it up, that is unusual."

"Not if it never left the palace," I say, cutting into the potatoes harder than I need to. "The prince seems awfully eager to find out how much I know about the theft."

Feliks stares. "What reason would the prince have to steal, though? He's already got everything he could possibly want."

"That I don't know," I say.

Behind us, the fire crackles into life, sending warmth across the kitchen. Sasha pours pails of water, filling the pots. My gaze wanders to the Peacekeeper. "We should get the keys now," I say.

"Do you have the soap with you?" he asks.

I nod. It's still tucked into my hat where I hid it last night. "But not the metal," I say. I still can't think of a reason someone would have taken the pick and yet not reported Katia and me to Warden Kirov.

"I can get the keys now," he says. "We can worry about the metal later. No sense in wasting a perfect opportunity."

I glance at the Peacekeeper standing guard by the door. He's taller than the door frame, almost as wide as the door itself, and his arms, folded in front of him, bulge so that the chessboard tattoo stretches and curves like an optical illusion. I hesitate, and my doubt must show on my face, because Feliks grins.

"Everyone else sees a problem, Valor. I see an opportunity. Trust me."

I wish I were stealing the keys myself, but the truth is I have no idea how. Somehow it makes me more nervous knowing that this Peacekeeper is the one who gave me my first infraction.

"I do trust you. I'm counting on you," I say. "I'll create a distraction in a minute. But are you going to peel *any* of these potatoes?"

"Valor." He lifts his hands and wiggles his fingers at me. His nails are dirty. "You can't possibly expect me to risk these valuable hands on anything so mundane as a paring knife."

My heart beats up into my throat at the thought of what we're going to do, but I smile. "Just tell me when."

The air in the kitchen is warm; the fire crackles and the water in the pots bubbles. Sasha is in the alcove now, scrubbing bowls in a long sink with Nicolai and Katia. The other two boys are carrying stacks of glistening wet bowls and spoons back to the ice hall in preparation for the evening meal. The job is all but finished.

Feliks glides away from me with a pan of peeled potatoes and whispers something in Sasha's ear. Sasha leans in and passes it on to Katia as Feliks slips away again.

"Move over." I jump. I'd been flitting back and forth between watching Feliks and eyeing the Peacekeeper, still standing like a statue in front of the doors. Natalia is behind me, holding a paring knife.

"Natalia," calls Nicolai, "can you come with me? We need to fire up the ovens and fetch more flour from the stores for bread."

Feliks, heading back my way with an empty pan, widens his eyes. This is our chance.

We heap the pans with potatoes and haul them toward the pots over the fire. I give Feliks a nod as we walk, and he returns it. I take a deep breath. Suddenly my insides feel unanchored, floating around in the middle of me.

I tip the contents of the pan into the pot. The water inside bubbles, sending steam into my face. I swipe back the tiny strands of hair sticking to my temples. Then I hook the handle of my pan into one of the handles on the side of the pot, and as Feliks leaps away, I throw my weight back, heaving the pot with me.

Boiling water sloshes over the top and slaps onto the floor, and the weight of it tips the whole vat, sending it crashing, pouring, spilling potatoes. I fall backward onto the rough tile, my hands hitting the floor where the hot water has spread. I cry out, feeling the stinging burn on my palms.

Around me, Katia and Sasha are making an unholy din, shouting my name. The floor is slick with water and slithering potatoes. The Peacekeeper rushes forward and heaves the huge pot upright. Feliks, who was nowhere to be seen, spins around the back of the Peacekeeper, knocks into him, and tangles himself as if he has slipped and fallen. The Peacekeeper pushes him away.

Water seeps into my trousers, and I scramble back out of the huge puddle.

"Valor! Your hands." Sasha kneels at my side, concern all over her face. My hands are throbbing, the skin on them red and scalded.

"I'm okay," I say, though tears fill my eyes.

The Peacekeeper stands over me. My sister looks up at him. "She needs help."

He reaches for his belt and I leap to my feet, panicking. He's going to discover that his keys are missing. "It's nothing, Sasha. Be quiet." My heart pounds, making the throb in my hands unbearable.

But instead the Peacekeeper retrieves the familiar pouch, and I stand there shaking as he marks me with an infraction and growls "Clean it up" before turning his back on us and walking away.

Katia grabs a small pan and scurries around collecting the spilled vegetables. Sasha and I hurry into the alcove where Feliks is arming himself with two cloths.

"Valor, let me see."

I hold out my hands, and he presses his lips together, then pulls his sleeve up. There's a pink scar running fat and shiny across his whole skinny forearm. I remember him rubbing at the same spot when he told me he'd worked in a forge.

"You'll be okay," he says to me.

He moves in close to Sasha, takes her hand, and presses a bunch of keys into her palm, taking care that they don't clink together. "Hurry," he whispers, then flits away and begins soaking up the spilled water with his cloths.

I pull my *ushanka* off with clumsy fingers, wincing as I try to free the soap from its hiding place. Sasha peeks around the corner and gives me a nod. We press back against the sink, crouching in the corner. I hold the block of soap steady as she pushes the blade of each key into it and makes an impression. I can hear each tiny noise the keys make as they move against each other, though she's taking care to keep them separated. The pain in my hands pulses in time with my heart.

A shadow falls over us—Sasha holding the keys and me holding the soap. I suck in a breath. Natalia stands there, arms crossed, smiling.

Nicolai arrives behind her, out of breath. He shakes his head helplessly, raising his hands.

"Valor," says Natalia. "Oh, Valor. I knew keeping you close would be a good idea."

CHAPTER 13

I get on my feet fast.

Natalia puts a warning finger to her lips.

"We can't all just stand here," says Nicolai in a desperate whisper.

She turns on him. "Then don't."

Out in the kitchen, Katia hurries about, transferring armfuls of vegetables to the cooking pots and casting worried glances at me. Feliks is over at the mountain of potatoes, working his way through it as though nothing has happened. Nicolai stares at Natalia like he's going to say something, then turns abruptly. His clothes are dusted with flour. He joins Feliks, and they both bow their heads over their work.

Natalia tilts her head at Sasha. "Best run, little girl, and return those keys to your thief. He needs to put them back before they're missed."

Sasha bites her lip, then nods miserably.

Natalia looks like the cat that got the cream. "I think it's time Valor and I had a little talk." She reaches carefully for the soap I'm still holding to avoid damage to the key marks.

Feliks rushes into the alcove. "Peacekeeper," he hisses, then darts away. Natalia snatches the soap, gives me a glare that tells me this is far from over, and, folding the key impressions into her furs, disappears into the main kitchen just as Peacekeeper Rurik's demon blocks the light in the entrance to the alcove. I plunge my hands into the sink, praying he doesn't notice how much I'm shaking.

"Come with me," he says. I have no choice but to walk away from Feliks, Katia, and Sasha, who are gathered over a growing pile of potato peels. My hands are on fire.

When it becomes clear that Peacekeeper Rurik is leading me to the tower again, my heart sinks even lower. He unlocks the door, but this time I look away. I can't bear the reminder of how close we were to a set of those keys.

In the tower, music comes from upstairs—thin, heartbreaking notes from a violin. I stand on the blue carpet, transfixed. I haven't heard music since I came here. I thought nothing of the chance to learn to play an instrument myself; I threw it away as though it meant nothing. I've never truly appreciated the privileges in my life. And not once in my life have I understood, until this moment, that if I don't hear music, I will miss it in the same place that I miss Mother and Father. It brings tears that are still blurring my eyes when the music stops and Prince Anatol walks down the stairs.

One glance from him and Peacekeeper Rurik moves to stand outside the door. The prince walks past me and closes it with a click. We're alone. Again.

"I hear all sorts of interesting things from Warden Kirov," he says as he moves to stand in front of me.

I swallow. There's a whirlwind of thoughts in my head— the keys, the pick. What does the warden know? What has she told the prince?

Anatol's eyes narrow. "I hear that I owe you my life. You saved me from the wolves. Didn't you?"

"Yes, Your Highness," I say. My voice is too high, on edge like a balanced knife.

He frowns at my use of the honorific, as if displeases him somehow. "You tried to kill me not so long ago, but then you saved me. Why is that?"

"I'm reformed now," I say. My hands are buzzing with pain. I should probably be more careful with what I say, but I want to get out of this tower as fast as I can.

The prince rubs his face and sighs, suddenly looking less like royalty and a lot younger. "Valor, if you shoot as well as I'm told you did at those wolves, then you can shoot well enough to have hit me at the parade. I don't think you were trying to kill me at all."

I stand rigid, trying not to look surprised. "No, I was. It—it's just that I had no choice last night because the warden threatened my sister. I didn't want to save you. I *had* to save you." My heart starts up an uncomfortable beat. I can't have him finding out why I'm here. He needs to believe I tried to kill him as revenge for locking my sister up.

"You're lying!" His eyes are wide now, his mouth set in a stubborn line. "I know something else about Warden Kirov. She said she'd let your sister out of the Black Hands if you saved me, but then she went back on her word. I was told."

Being scared is making me angry, and I don't know what he wants me to say. "Told by *who*?" I yell, throwing my hands up.

His face changes when he sees my hands. I would think it was concern, only it can't be. He takes hold of my wrists and bends his head over my palms. "What happened?"

I wrench my hands away. "Nothing."

"It's not nothing," he says. "Come with me." He flings the door open and glares at me furiously. Peacekeeper Rurik stands like a statue outside in the snow. I already have one inky black mark on my forehead, so I have no choice but to stomp out into the cold.

Prince Anatol marches off behind the tower to where it curves around and joins the great wall. There's a drift of snow piled high in the corner. "Come here," he says. Then His Royal Highness Prince Anatol of Demidova takes my hands carefully and drops to his knees in the snow, pulling me with him, and presses my palms to the soft, powdered snow gathered by the wind against the wall.

Immediately, cold crystals begin to melt against my hot skin, and the burn begins to cool. Nothing has ever felt so good. Why is he doing this?

"You know Sasha's innocent," he says.

I try to pull my hands away. "No. No, I—I don't know anything." I shake my head, willing him to believe me.

He stares at me intently, his voice low. "You do. You've talked to your sister. She's told you she's innocent, and now you're trying to work it all out. I know you are. Why won't you just tell me?"

I tug back against his grip on my wrists, pulling away from him. He stole the music box himself. He's trying to find out how much I know—to protect himself. I have to get Sasha away before he finds some way to get rid of both of us for good.

"If you don't stop questioning me, I will beg Princess Anastasia to do something," I say. My voice wavers, but I stare defiance at him.

His mouth is a furious line, but I see what's in his eyes. It's fear.

I push up to my knees and then my feet, taking handfuls of snow with me. "I mean it. She's shown mercy already. She got Sasha out of the Black Hands. I'll tell her every-thing, and she'll help Sasha and me." I squeeze the snow in my hands to slush, and it drips through my fingers.

"If you know what's good for you, don't bring my sis-ter into this." The prince's eyes flash a warning, but it's too late—I've already seen how the very idea of it scares him.

"Then leave me alone," I say. "And leave my sister alone too."

I turn and run, leaving the prince down on his knees in the snow.

CHAPTER 14

I take a few more steps, fresh snow squeaking under my boots, and then stop some distance from the laundry. My heart beats even faster the second I stop running, as though it's just caught up and realized that I threatened a prince.

I hear Prince Anatol saying something behind me, and Peacekeeper Rurik answering. I bite my lip and spin around, expecting the Peacekeeper to be right behind me, but he and the prince are still talking. And I have nowhere to run. So I stare at them, trying to figure out what's going to happen to me now. Snow starts to fall in fine flurries, hazing the outline of the prince and dotting the Peacekeeper's black uniform with white.

They both look at me, and then Peacekeeper Rurik bows to Anatol and starts across the snow toward me. The prince sweeps his cloak around himself, goes back into the tower, and slams the door.

When Rurik reaches me, he points to one of the small buildings clustered between the laundry and the boys' cell-block. I swallow. I know one is the forge, and one is the store. The other has thin, high windows—the only building in Tyur'ma that has windows at all.

I bite back the urge to ask him where he's taking me this time. I know he wouldn't answer. Instead I march behind him, my boots sinking into the enormous prints he leaves on the ground, and I try to calm every twitchy nerve in my body. Is the prince watching me from his tower? I won't give him the satisfaction of seeing me turn around to check. I blink snowflakes from my lashes and focus on the tattoos twining up the back of the Peace-keeper's arms.

"In," Peacekeeper Rurik says. We've reached the high-windowed building. He opens the door and I hesitate, peer-ing into the room, my heart still pounding. Natural light slants in from each of the windows, though they're so high all I can see is white sky. Rows of beds stand against the walls on either side of the room, all made up tightly with white sheets like the one I have hidden beneath my mat-tress in my cell. It's the infirmary.

A fire blazes high in a wide fireplace at the back of the room, though none of the beds are in use. There are two other rooms branching off from this one. The doors are open a little, but I can't see into them.

"In," says Peacekeeper Rurik in a tone that tells me he won't say it a third time. He pushes me forward, and I step onto a mat on the tiled floor. I smell oil lamps and soap and herbs I don't have names for.

One of the other doors opens and a woman appears. She's shorter than I am, her hair pulled back into one long braid that suddenly reminds me of my mother and makes my chest ache. Behind her are two beds, and sitting on one of them is a huddle of brown furs.

The woman nods to Peacekeeper Rurik, and he leaves, shutting the door to the infirmary and closing out the cold.

"Come through," says the woman. I hesitate, looking around warily, and then walk through into the next room. It's smaller, with only the two beds, a sink, and a shelf brimming with jars of herbs and pastes and liquids, each labeled in a tiny looping script.

"Name?" she asks.

"Valor Raisayevna," I tell her. I used to be proud of it. Now my stomach clenches. But the woman doesn't react.

The mass on one of the beds moves. It's the girl with the eye patch—the one who saved me that night when I almost fell from the ledge on my way to find Sasha's cell. The one Katia told me had tried to escape. Her name is Mila. I can't stop myself from checking her hands. One is scrunched tight into her furs. The other sleeve lies in her lap, a gaping hole at the end of it where her hand should be. I swallow.

The woman gestures at the other bed. "I'm Dr. Lenina. Sit." She has a quiet voice, and she doesn't look at me the way Warden Kirov does.

I perch on the edge of the bed. "Why am I here?"

She smiles—the first real smile I've seen on an adult since I came here. "This is an infirmary. I presume you can tell me why you're here?"

I'd almost forgotten that my hands hurt. Now that the doctor mentions it, though, a fresh wave of stinging washes over my palms. When I lift my hands up, they're red and starting to blister in places.

The doctor nods and busies herself with something in the sink. "Take your coat off and we'll have a look."

I don't understand. Is the prince scared that I'll show Princess Anastasia my injury? Is he going to leave me alone, stop questioning me now? I've played a dangerous card, threatening a prince, but . . . have I won? I bend my fingers, wincing, and struggle to do as the doctor says. If Natalia hadn't taken the key impressions, it might all have been worth it.

"Here. Let me help you."

I pull away from her; I can't stop myself.

She pauses and presses her lips together. "You know, I always wanted to be a children's doctor. And where better to do it than where I'm most needed? Warden Kirov is very dedicated to her job, and to the royal family. But believe me, Valor, I am equally dedicated to mine."

She moves toward me again and unbuttons my furs with deft fingers, then gently slips them over my shoulders and lays them on the bed. Then she takes my hands and inspects them, frowning and turning them this way and that. Her own hands are cool and careful.

"I'm going to make a salve and bandage them." She turns to the other girl. "Mila, I'll make yours at the same time. Wait here."

Dr. Lenina crosses to the other door. I hear clinking as she gathers supplies in the next room. Opposite me, Mila sits, her good eye staring steadily at me. I haven't seen her since the night she pulled me back onto the ledge.

I clear my throat. "Thank you for what you did for me."

"Think nothing of it." I'd forgotten how low her voice is. Soft, though, like gravel under water.

"But I do. I think a lot of it," I say, ashamed that I haven't sought her out before, that I haven't thanked her properly for putting herself at odds with the other prisoners for a complete stranger. "I— I'm sorry about us having no roof that night because of me. My sister was up in that cell, and I wouldn't have gotten to her if you hadn't helped me."

I think about Sasha now, back in the kitchens with Natalia. I'm itching to know what's happening in there.

In the room next door, glass clinks on glass, and the doctor says something to herself.

Mila leans forward. The cuff of her coat folds in, empty where her hand should be. "There are people in your work detail you should steer clear of," she says, as though she's read my mind.

The pulse in my neck leaps. "I've been trying to."

"Not hard enough, I bet." She shakes her head. "You can get yourself into a lot of trouble mixing with the wrong people. My advice? Don't make friends in here. You don't know who you can trust."

The doctor's footsteps sound on the tiles.

"Who? Who can't I trust?" I say.

"The warden has spies. And she's not the only one."

Dr. Lenina knocks the door open with her elbow, her hands full of bandages and bowls. She hands Mila a bowl of ointment that smells of mint and something darker. Mila places it on the bed beside her.

The doctor takes my hands and smears the contents of another bowl over my skin. It tingles, then soothes, taking the fire out of the burns. I feel my whole body relax, even if my mind can't. She wraps soft white bandages around my palms and each of my fingers.

I let her work. Over her shoulder, I see Mila dip her fingers into the paste in her bowl. She lifts the eye patch from the ruined socket that was once her eye, before she crossed Warden Kirov. I try not to stare at what the warden did to her. It speaks of a cruelty I've only seen the surface of.

While the doctor finishes dressing my hands, Mila shuffles down from the bed, places her bowl in the sink, and leaves, as though her being in the infirmary is a regular occurrence. How long has it been since she tried to escape?

I move to follow her, eager to find out more, but Dr. Lenina protests. "Valor, instructions have to be followed. You are to rest here for a while."

I glance at the door. "I need to get back to work. My sister—"

She puts her hand on my shoulder and guides me back onto the bed. I wilt a little under her gentleness. But I have to get to Sasha.

"You're not going anywhere," says Dr. Lenina, and for the first time she sounds like she won't take no for an answer. She makes me lie down, and when she smooths my hair back from my forehead, the kindness undoes me altogether. I close my eyes as tears fill them. I've tried so hard, but doubt has seeped into me like the cold. I don't feel like a girl who believes she can rescue her sister at all.

❧

I wake slowly, the sheet soft against my cheek. For a moment, I'm back at home, with Father working downstairs in his study. I hear Sasha arguing some point of law or court politics with him. Mother is sharpening hunting knives in the kitchen, which sends the housekeeper wild with annoyance. I smile, and then I remember where I am. My eyes snap open. There's a blanket over me. I push it off as I sit up. The door is open, and the light from the ward is dim. I jump up, my hands swathed in bandages.

When Dr. Lenina releases me from the infirmary, the sky is darkening to a bruised purple. The prison grounds are covered in a fresh coat of snow, bare and clean of footprints, empty of inmates. Up on the wall, a Peacekeeper is lighting the nighttime torches. A lone wolf calls, long and lonely, raising the hair on my arms.

I hurry toward the ice hall for the evening meal, my breath huffing in icy crystals. As I pass the forge, where the air still smells of hot metal, there's a soft crunch behind me. I spin around, alert and jumpy, pulling myself back into the Valor who exists outside of the infirmary. The soft sheets are gone, and the bitter cold is back. There's nothing behind me, though; only the snow, sparkling and deadly in the growing firelight.

I rush on past the store, a low building trimmed with windswept icicles as long as my arm in places. A scuffling noise followed by a snap makes me drag in a breath, scanning behind me again. There are eyes on me. I feel them. I sense them as though there were a wolf from beyond the wall stalking me. My skin prickles.

The strange underwater glow of the ice hall is just visible. I run for it, into the shadows of the boys' cellblock. Feet pound the ground behind me. I don't look back. I push myself forward and someone hits me from the side, knocking me into the wall. I yelp, kicking out and almost losing my balance. Hands grab me and throw my back against the wall, rattling my teeth.

Something sharp pushes into the soft part of my neck underneath my jaw.

"Quiet," says Natalia. "So." She leans right into my face. "When are we escaping, Valor?"

I shake my head. The plan was for Sasha and me. I've already added Katia and Feliks, which means I'm already trusting more people than I wanted to with my plans. And I don't trust Natalia at all. "There is no *we*. You're the one with the key impressions."

Her face hardens. "I can't just open the gates and stroll out across the plains. So I want to know what you're planning. And I want to know when we're leaving." She slides one hand down my arm and snatches my bandaged left hand. I try to pull away, but she slams me against the wall again. The back of my head hits stone. A cold trickle runs down my neck, and I realize the sharp thing at my throat is an icicle.

Natalia squeezes my fingers, crushing the tender skin. I grit my teeth as tears spring into my eyes. She sighs, like it's my fault. "Do you really think I'm going to bother making a new plan myself when it's clear you already have one? Either you get me out of here too, or I'm going straight to Warden Kirov, and you and your precious sister will never escape Tyur'ma. I'm sure she'd give me a pretty nice reward for information like this. But maybe you think she likes you. Maybe you think she'd believe you over me. It's your choice, Valor."

"Stop." My voice is twisted up with pain, but she doesn't let go of my hands. "I have a p-plan. There's a tunnel, under the tower. But I need the keys to check the escape route first. And you took them."

She finally lets go of my hands. I gasp, curling forward over them. She drops the icicle to the ground and kicks snow over it.

"Why can't we just leave?" she asks. "We should go now."

"I told you. Without the keys, we can't get out. I was going to find the escape route. I know it's under the tower somewhere, but I have to find it. What if we all get into the tower and then we can't get out? What if the tunnels are blocked? It has to be perfect."

"You really had this all planned out, didn't you?" Natalia sounds almost impressed. "Are you sure there are even tunnels at all?"

I hug my stinging hands to myself. "Yes. I've seen them on old maps that belong to my father. But you took the molds I was going to use for the keys, and now—"

She brings up her hand and releases something from her fist so that it dangles in front of me. A set of silver keys.

I straighten in astonishment, my heart leaping up.

"It's all taken care of. See? I want to work with you. The Peacekeeper was none the wiser after Feliks returned his keys. Between him and your sister, they had the whole thing figured out in no time. And now I'm giving these to you. I'm trusting you to get me out of here." She holds out the bunch of keys and I look at them, perfect and silver, my whole life dangling right there with them in Natalia's hand.

"Take them. Find this escape route tonight. I want to get out of here tomorrow, and you're going to make sure that happens."

I try to stop my hand from shaking as I take the keys. My fingers are clumsy as I hide them in the compartment in my boot. Natalia disappears into the shadows, and I walk on trembling legs to the ice hall.

A Peacekeeper questions me. I show him my bandaged hands as an excuse. I only want to see Sasha. And even though I'm too late for food and we get marched back to the cellblock right away, it's enough just to see her face. I walk in silence beside her, and it makes me feel better to know she's all right.

It's not until sometime after we're in our cells, the lights dim and the cellblock silent, that Katia climbs up to my bunk.

"Here," she whispers, pushing something into my hands. I scramble up, my back against the wall. There's a torn lump of bread and some chunks of cheese in my grasp. I look at her in surprise. "Thank you." I start to shovel it into my mouth, only now realizing how hungry I am.

She sits next to me, her long, thin legs sticking straight out over the end of the bed. "After what happened today . . . well, this is serious, isn't it? We're really leaving here. And I can't let everyone else take all the risks when I take none myself. It isn't right."

"But, Katia, you risk everything all the time just by sharing a cell with me. If Warden Kirov found out—"

"Well, we'd better make sure she doesn't, then. There's no going back. Not now that we have keys. Not when Natalia and Nicolai are coming too."

I swallow my mouthful. "Nicolai?"

"He can't stay now. Practically his whole work detail is escaping. Think what the warden would do to him. And he helped so much, Valor. He did exactly what Sasha and Feliks said."

"How *did* the keys get made?" I push the last of the food into my mouth, trying to chew slowly.

"Sasha and Feliks. You should have seen them." Her eyes shine with pride. "Sasha got Feliks to return the keys. Then she sent Nicolai to the forge with a story about putting in an order for some new silver cutlery for the warden.

Apparently, some of the old set got . . . damaged." Katia grins wickedly.

"You stole the warden's cutlery to melt down and make the keys?" I can't believe all this went on without me there. Feliks and Sasha are quite the team.

She nods, grinning at the memory. "It was all Sasha's idea. I never dared to hope. I never let myself think that I could leave here. But when I see how determined you are, and I hear your sister standing up to Natalia, telling her she has to clear it with you if she wants to join us, I can't help myself." She presses her hand over her chest and takes a breath.

I shake my head in wonder. "I wish I'd been there. My sister has a way with words that I'll never have. But I don't think she knew exactly how Natalia planned on clearing it with me." I reach down and pull the blade of one key from its hiding place in my boot.

"You have them now?" Her smile falters.

I tell her about my little meeting with Natalia. Her eyes are round when I finish.

"You have to go out of here tonight? By yourself? It's too dangerous."

"If I don't, Natalia will turn me in to Warden Kirov. And if that happens, I won't be the only one who pays. I have to go tonight."

After that Katia is silent, worry turning her mouth down and filling her eyes with fear. The cold and the silence seep into every part of me, and so when I give her a nod and climb down from the bunk sometime later, every brush of my furs across the iron frame sounds like the grating of the roof being rolled back.

I ease the folded sheet I took from the laundry out from under the mattress and secure it in the waistband of my trousers. I press my face to the bars, looking left and right. The cellblock is full of deep, flickering shadows. Sasha's cell is as dark and soundless as all the others.

Mila was wrong about not trusting anybody. I see it for the first time since I came here, and in spite of what happened with Natalia. I can trust my sister. I can trust my friends. That's why Mila never made it out of here. And it's why I will.

I slip the keys out of my boot, separating the cell door key from the others, muffling the rest of the bunch with my bandaged hand. My fingers hurt where Natalia squeezed them, but whatever Dr. Lenina put on my hands is wonderful, because all I feel is a dull pulsing.

I look over my shoulder at Katia's tense face.

I hold my breath to stop my hand from shaking and press the key forward a fraction of an inch at a time, as though letting it touch the sides of the lock will make lightning strike me.

I turn the key. The lock on my cell door opens.

CHAPTER 15

I grasp the bars and push the door. It swings open slowly, throwing long striped shadows across the wall. Katia sits rigid on the bed, her hands pressed over her mouth. I blow out my breath silently and step onto the narrow ledge outside the cell. The gulf on the other side seems wider and deeper than in the daytime, when girls rush past it to get into the food line.

I peek into the cell next to ours. The girls are dark shapes, huddled on their bunks. They breathe quietly, exhausted from the day's work. I grasp the keys, take one last look at Katia, and sneak away into the shadows that line the cells.

My eyes strain to pick out the sleeping figures in each cell as I move along the row. When I make it to the steps that lead down to the door, I'm lightheaded from taking shallow breaths. I make myself breathe deeply as I hug the wall, picking my way down the steps. I hurry past the lone torch, tensed in anticipation of any inmates seeing me.

Someone shouts out a single word that freezes me and sends the pulse in my neck bounding. I wait and wait, but nothing happens. Someone calling out in her sleep. At the narrow door to the cellblock, I listen. Is there a Peacekeeper stationed outside? Or are they patrolling the grounds right now?

There's no way to find out but to unlock the door. I'm shaking, poised to run back to my cell. I untuck the white sheet, drape it around myself so it covers my dark clothes, and twist the key.

An icy wind blows in and makes my heart race even faster. But I keep my eyes glued to the crack. There's no Peacekeeper outside. The grounds are empty, the snow crisp and white. Torches burn brightly all around the top of the wall. Something moves, blocking one of the lights. A Peacekeeper walks slowly along the battlements where I saw Prince Anatol arguing with his sister. Where I shot the arrows that saved his life.

Atop the wall, the Peacekeeper walks past, and I see my chance. I slip out of the smallest possible gap I can create with the door and close it, wincing at the tiny noise it makes as it shuts. Then I crouch in the snow and run, praying the white sheet pulled over me is enough to stop my movement from catching the Peacekeeper's eye.

The air is diamond-hard, with a cold that makes my lungs hitch. I think about Sasha to stop myself from running back to my cell, and hurry into the shadows by the boys' block. The wind has blown drifts of snow against the walls, and my boots sink deep into them. Cold surrounds my legs, but at least with the sheet pulled over my head and around everything but my eyes I blend into the background. If I'm caught now, I don't know what Warden Kirov will do to me.

I wade along, keeping to the shadows, hoping the wind will blow a covering of snow onto my tracks. High above on the wall, the Peacekeeper turns the far corner, heading toward the mines. I take a few breaths, trying in vain to quiet the thump of my heart, and then I run into the open, heading for the tower. The wolves call to each other out on the plains, but there's another sound that sends my pulse racing higher: boots on the snow.

Across the grounds, a Peacekeeper opens the gate in the wall, the same one that leads to the cage where Feliks and I stood the day we arrived. It's the woman with the cruel-beaked eagle tattoos. She hasn't seen me, but if I keep running, she will.

I drop to the ground on my stomach, burrowing into the snow and pulling the sheet flat above me. Icy cold reaches up though my clothes into my body. The Peacekeeper strides diagonally across the grounds, heading for the ice hall. I shiver, my teeth chattering. I can hardly tell whether fear or cold is making me shake. As she reaches the closest point to me on her path, I hold my breath and scrunch my eyes shut.

When I open them, she's gone. I let the breath out and scan the grounds, waiting as long as I can as the cold seeps into my bones. Shuffling around, I check behind me. Nothing.

I stagger up, pull my sheet around me, though it's wet and weighted with snow now, and run for the tower. The keys are heavy in my hands, my fingers numb and clumsy with cold. I try to feed the key into the curved door, but the bunch falls into the snow. My bandaged fingers are frantic, scuffing snow out of the way. My breath races away from me as I try to tame it.

I snatch the bunch of keys, jostling them together as I try to wrench the one I need away from the others. Finally I jam it into the lock, too far gripped by panic to think straight. I twist it and push the door, falling through in a tangle of wet sheet.

I lie in the dark on the plush carpet for a second, then tear the sheet off my legs and shove the door closed again. I listen hard, but the only sounds are the muffled calls of the wolves. Inside, the tower is silent and dark, solid and windowless.

I feel along the wall until I knock into a table and put my hands down on an oil lamp. After three failed attempts with my bandaged fingers, I have to unwrap my thumbs and two fingers on each hand. My skin is red and angry, and I try not to look as I light the lamp.

The spiral stairs are on the far side of the room. I kick the sheet into a ball and shove it under the table, then hurry to the stairs, this time going down to the level below ground. The light from the lamp is so soft and localized that I almost run into the door before I see it. Solid wood braced with iron bands. I stare at it, panic pinching every muscle in my back tight, before I think to check my keys. One by one I feed them into the lock, trying to hold the lamp steady. When I get to the last one on the ring, I hold it tight in my hand as though I can squeeze it into the right shape just by wanting it enough. I take a breath and feed the blade in.

It doesn't fit.

I sink back onto the step, watching the little flame glow yellow in my hand. If I let myself sit here, I will never get up. I'll let the avalanche of hopeless feelings thunder down and crush me. And a Peacekeeper will catch me. So I force my legs to push me up. I'm going to look for a key. There's an office upstairs, and I'm going to find the key for this door.

I keep telling myself this over and over as I put one foot in front of the other up the stairs. I pause on the ground floor, listening, but Tyur'ma is silent. I check the blue-carpeted room quickly, then the room with the collection of chairs around the table, and then the room with the music stand—minus its violin today—but there's nothing in any of the spots where a person would naturally keep a key.

In the room at the top of the tower, I keep low, shielding my lamp from the window. I have no idea how long the Peacekeeper on the battlements will stay out there, and the only way back is through this room. I'll have to be quick. Quick and quiet. He could return at any moment.

I put the lamp on the floor by the desk and search its surface. Documents, ink, nothing remotely key-shaped. For an instant I have a rogue thought that I'll find the actual music box itself, stolen and transported here. No one would think to look for it in a prison. My heart beats wildly at the idea of it.

But the drawers only turn up more papers and a ledger. No music box. And no big clue that proves the prince stole it. I'm sliding a drawer shut when something stops me dead. A letter addressed to Warden Kirov with the royal seal on it. I hold it close to the lamp and see the muddle of black lettering inside through the parchment of the envelope. At the bottom, in a haughty-looking slanted hand, is a name: Prince Anatol.

I bite my bottom lip hard. Outside on the battlements, there's a sound. I stuff the letter inside my coat and search the last drawer in the desk with frenzied hands. There are no keys. I swing around, wildly searching the room. It has to be here somewhere.

The hidden panel door opens, admitting a freezing wind. I throw myself under the desk, stomping my boot down on the oil lamp and drawing myself into the space as tightly as I can in a horrible, twisted form of the hide-and-seek game I used to play with Sasha. The thump of my blood in my body fills the space with me, and the smell of singed fur reaches my nose as the Peacekeeper steps inside. The panel slides shut. Footsteps cross the room. I pull my knees so hard against my chest that I can hardly breathe.

The steps go down the staircase. I sit frozen, my eyes wide and tight in the dark. After what seems like forever, the door at the bottom of the tower opens and closes. My head drops onto my knees and I shake. But I don't have time to waste being scared, so I pull myself out from under the desk. Light from the clear night sky throws a thin beam through the single narrow window and across the middle of the desk.

Which, now that I stare at it, seems oddly deeper than the drawers suggest. I pull open the narrow drawer in the middle again. I was right—it's far too shallow for the depth of the desk. I push my fingers inside, feeling around the underside.

There's nothing but smooth wood. My finger slips over a knot in the wood, and a false panel springs down to reveal a velvet-lined tray. I let out a breath in a rush. On the tray, there's a gold clasp in the shape of a fist and a thick gold ring bearing the royal seal. And two copies of a black key with matching blades and the same bow at the head of each, shaped like a thin bread twist from the bakery in the town square.

I almost jump into the air. Instead, I tuck my trailing bandages into my sleeves, pick up one of the keys, and put everything else back as it was. Taking the lamp with me, I hurry down the staircase. My eyes are trained on the door, watching for Peacekeepers as I relight the lamp and rush back to the lower-level door. It has to fit. This *has* to be the key.

I slip the key in, pause for a moment, and turn it. The lock opens with a well-oiled click. I rest my damp forehead against the cold iron on the door, tired out from tension and sudden relief. No sounds come from behind the door, but I press my ear to it anyway. Nothing.

I turn the handle and hold the lamp in front of me, not able to stop the little cry that comes out. Ahead of me, stretching off into the blackness, is a maze of tunnels, each one tall and wide enough for two men to walk through side by side. There are four openings, all of them arched overhead and tiled in ancient mosaics.

Three of the tunnels are dark, a black and murky cold pressing out from them, cobwebs hanging across their mouths. The fourth one, directly in front of me, is clean and dimly lit with oil lamps that illuminate the once-bright tiles of the mosaics around them. It stretches away in a straight line as far as I can see. This is how the prince arrives here and disappears without warning. He never comes by carriage, except for the time he came on the cart with Peacekeeper Rurik. Warden Kirov said the prince wanted to speak with him to learn about the prison—the same Peacekeeper who just *happened* to transport me from the palace to the prison.

A damp, earthy smell fills the airless space, but there's a hint of oil too. I close my eyes and call to mind the secret maps I saw in Father's study. They confirm this tunnel leads to the city. But the warden won't realize I know that.

We'll sweep all the cobwebs away tomorrow night when we escape, and even if Warden Kirov does by some chance check the tunnels, she won't know for sure which one we've taken.

I peer ahead cautiously—there's a chance someone else could be here—and walk a little way down the lit tunnel. Tomorrow, we'll run. And this is how it will feel to have Sasha's hand in mine as we run away from cells and Peacekeepers and work in the mines. Away from Warden Kirov and Tyur'ma and Prince Anatol. I imagine how bright her eyes will get as we near the city. It will be dangerous getting to the docks, and maybe we'll be hungry and maybe we'll be cold, but we'll be free.

I stop walking. I have to wait until tomorrow for this. I have to get back to my cell now.

I lock the door behind me, run up the tower staircase, and return the key to exactly the right position on its velvet-lined tray. Downstairs, I pull my sheet out from its hiding place, relieved that I hid it and that the Peacekeeper on wall duty didn't see it in the dark, and place the oil lamp back on its little table, snuffing out the light. I brace myself to go through it all again, back across the grounds without being seen, my heart pounding out of my chest.

Keys in hand, ready to lock the tower again, I take one last, hurried glance around. Everything is as I found it. I open the door a crack. The wind blows along the silent prison grounds, rippling the snow. My tracks have been covered while I was inside. A light dusting of fresh snow falls through the opening I've made. I tug the sheet around myself and step outside, closing the door quietly.

"Hello, Valor," says Warden Kirov.

CHAPTER 16

The shock of her voice hits me like a bucket of freezing water to the face. I stagger back and pull in an icy lungful of air so fast it constricts my throat. Warden Kirov stands with a Peacekeeper on either side of her and holds out her immaculate gray glove.

I stare at it for a few seconds before she makes an impatient noise, and I realize she's demanding the keys. I look at my hand, though it hardly feels like my own right now, and then I reach out and give her the bunch. She examines each key in turn. Then she narrows her eyes. "I think we'll conduct this interview in the forge." The Peacekeepers move to stand on either side of me, but my legs don't want to work. They're made of ice, and if I move, they'll shatter like my heart.

They half carry me to the forge. The building is empty, but torches burn along the walls. Coal fires smolder in pits.

The Peacekeepers haul me to an anvil, and I wait, trying to stand up straight and not crumple and cry. Then they all face me. Behind them, great iron tools hang along the walls: pliers and hammers and black tongs, pokers and chains and rows and rows of iron cuffs, all dull and dark in the half light.

"I'm going to ask you two questions, Valor. Just two," says Warden Kirov. The side of her face is lit by a torch, casting one eye in orange and the other in shadow. "Where did you get these?" She holds up my keys. "And what were you doing in the tower?"

It's warm with the smell of hot metal in the forge, but her words are like black ice, cold and slippery, tricky with menace. A shiver slithers down my back.

"I—I stole them from a Peacekeeper," I say.

Warden Kirov's mouth flattens into a thin line. "None of my Peacekeepers are missing any keys. And none of my Peacekeepers' keys are silver. That's the last lie I'm going to accept from you, Valor."

I swallow. I can't let her find out anyone else was involved. "I stole soap and made impressions of the Peace-keeper's keys, then I put his keys back and made those keys right here in the forge." I say it in a rush, feeling heat push up my neck and spread across my face.

"You expect me to believe that you managed all that by yourself? Without any help?" Warden Kirov takes a step forward, and I back up into the anvil. She crosses the room, selects an iron poker from the wall, and walks slowly and deliberately over to the fire pit, letting the hooked tip of the poker trail across the floor. The fire burns low, and she thrusts the poker into it, stirring up the coals so they spit and glow orange.

A bead of sweat runs down the small of my back.

"Let's try the other question for now, shall we? Tell me what you were doing in the tower."

My mind flips about like a fish out of water. I can't tear my eyes off the warden as she slowly builds up the fire, raking the poker over the hot coals. I have to tell her something, but she can't find out I know about the tunnels.

"I was trying to kill the prince," I blurt out. It's the only confession I can think of, and I'm already in prison for that very thing. "I knew he was always in the tower. I saw him at the window, and he made the Peacekeepers take me there so he could question me. I thought he'd be there or that I—that I could hide and wait for him. He put my sister in here and now he hates me, and he won't stop until I'm dead or he is." My words trip over one another, spilling out of me in a rush.

Warden Kirov pulls the poker from the fire and examines the tip of it, now glowing a dull orange. My hands throb with the memory of the hot water searing them. She looks across at me, and I push farther back, my feet scrabbling on the coal shards littering the floor. The letter I stole slips out of my coat and drops in front of me. Warden Kirov nods to one of the Peacekeepers, who picks it up and hands it to her. She reads the front, her name written in the slanting hand that she must know belongs to the prince, and frowns. Of course. It's sealed. She hasn't read it yet. But neither have I.

She examines the seal but doesn't open it, and I itch to run forward to read the lines written on that page. She sees the prince's name through the paper like I did, and then abruptly shoves the poker back into the fire so hard it makes me jump.

"Lock her in solitary," she snaps. She strides to the door, then pauses. "No—chain her up in here. She won't be going back to the cellblock."

I jolt forward, then falter.

Warden Kirov notices. "Well, cells can't hold you anymore, can they, Valor? So we'll just have to think of something else." Judging by her grim smile, she's already thought of the "something else." And I'm not going to like it.

She sweeps out of the forge. I stare after her as the Peacekeepers fasten cold, heavy iron around my wrists and ankles and feed chains through the cuffs. I'm fastened by both sets of chains to the huge anvil in the middle of the room. When they leave, I sag to the floor, weighted down and so drained that I feel like I'll never move again. The warden will report to the prince. He'll find out I stole his letter.

For a while I sit, pinned by the iron, watching as the torches grow dim. My eyes get heavy, and then I jolt awake. The warden didn't believe I could have done this on my own. So what would she do when she left here? Who would she go to?

⚬∽ ᎒ℂ ∼⚬

"Get up."

I blink in the watery daylight, dragging my hands in to my body and then remembering, as the chains clank, what happened last night. I got caught. I lost the keys. I failed.

Peacekeeper Rurik stands over me, holding the keys to my cuffs. My arms and legs are stiff with cold as I stand. He releases me from the chains and leads me out into the prison grounds. It's snowing lightly. Lazy, delicate flakes drop gently from the sky. Inmates stand in rows outside the cellblocks, some of them shivering, all of them huffing misty breath that rises into the pale morning.

I see Nicolai, but not Feliks. His mouth is pressed tightly together. I scan for Sasha and Katia, but there are too many other girls. The warden stands in the middle of the grounds, her hands behind her back as though she's about to deliver a speech. In between her and the rows of prisoners, out on the expanse of fresh snow, are two tiny versions of the ice hall. These, though, have domed roofs, as though a shimmering, translucent ball has been cut in half and placed on the ground.

The one closest to me has an opening and a stack of huge ice blocks next to it in the snow. The Peacekeeper at my back pushes me forward. Warden Kirov moves aside, and then I see. I see what she's going to do to me, because she's already done it to someone else.

Inside the other dome, a figure huddles on the ground. Thick ice distorts the image, but I see the big, dark eyes, and it breaks my heart. Sasha. She's totally encased in ice.

Warden Kirov addresses the gathered prisoners. "No doubt you've heard by now that your friend Valor stole keys and left her cell last night. I've assembled you here this morning to show you what happens to those who cannot obey rules. Those who think rules apply only to other people. *Those*"—she pauses and looks at Sasha, who is shuddering on the ground, her arms rigid around her knees—"who aid others who break the rules, or even those who look the other way." She walks up and down the ranks of prisoners. "As you go about your work today, think about your own behavior. Think about the behavior of others, and how selfish acts can have disastrous consequences." She holds her arm out to Sasha as she finishes the sentence.

A tear freezes on my cheek. Warden Kirov is right. I deserve to be punished. I've put everyone I came in contact with in Tyur'ma in danger, and I'm no closer to saving my sister. All I've done is put her in more danger. She's suffering now, and it's my fault. I feel it like pain, physical and real in my chest.

The only hope I can cling to is that Warden Kirov believed me when I said I was trying to kill the prince. That she's punishing me for that and for escaping the cellblock. That she doesn't know I found the tunnels.

The inmates lined up in the snow stand still, some of them huddled in their furs with only their downcast eyes showing. None of them look at me. The warden walks back to the open ice dome, and the Peacekeeper pushes me farther forward. "Make no mistake, though," the warden says, her voice carrying across the cold, clear morning. "This was not an escape." She pauses. "There *is* no escape from Tyur'ma."

With that, she gives a curt nod to the Peacekeeper, and he thrusts me through the gap and into the dome. Immediately the cold presses down on me. I clench my fists, trying to keep my breathing even as he places the first ice block over the entrance. After that, I don't watch as each block is piled up, sealing me inside the ice. The wind cuts down, sounds are muted, and the world is restricted to warped images. Another Peacekeeper approaches and launches something at the ice. I lurch back just as a thick metal spike breaks through. When it's pulled out, there's a hole in the ice. He does this in several other places, and in each spot bitterly cold air whistles through the hole left behind. I crouch and bury my face in my mittens so I don't have to look.

When I raise my head, I'm trapped in a bubble of freezing air. Already I'm shivering hard. How long has Sasha been out here? While I was chained inside the warm forge feeling sorry for myself, she was being questioned by Warden Kirov and then punished.

A rush of shame pulses through me. I made her believe I could lead her out of here. I gave her hope. She trusted me.

I let my head drop onto my knees and shiver and refuse to look up even when the rest of the inmates start their workday and orders are shouted and boots stomp right past me. I'm rigid with cold, my teeth chattering so hard it hurts, when I look up again. The prison grounds are empty. Everyone is working. The sun is arcing up toward its peak in the sky, though it's hard to believe it ever warms the land below it.

Sasha is slumped on the ground. I watch her for a moment while my heart tries to pump blood around my sluggish body. I get to my knees and hammer on the ice, and then I stand and start shouting. She stirs. "Sasha, get up. You have to get up. We have to move," I scream at the ice.

I jump up and down on numb feet. "Get up. Get up *now*, Sasha." Suddenly I know that if she doesn't move, she will die. If that happens, it will destroy me. "*Move!*"

She shifts. I throw my arms and legs out as I jump up and down, yelling that she has to do the same. It takes her forever to haul herself to her knees and then to stumble to her feet.

I think her mouth moves, but I can't hear anything. I shake my head.

"It hurts." The words come faintly.

"I know. But we have to move. We'll freeze if we don't."

And so she does, copying my movements, and I know that even when I'm tired I can't stop, because she will too. We stamp and jump, but it's so cold, and I'm so tired that I only want to sleep.

Thoughts creep into my head about curling up in the snow and resting, just for a little while. I stare at the ripples and twists the ice makes on Sasha as she swings her arms. The sun peaks and slowly starts to descend again. I think about clawing my way out of here, kicking the ice until it breaks or I do. And after that, I stop thinking anything at all. I'm so cold, and the only way I know my feet are still moving is because I can see them.

Eventually I notice I'm shuffling around in a circle. I can't move fast anymore—even if I wanted to. The ice hall is lit for the night, and the other prisoners are inside. My stomach growls and cramps.

Sasha has stopped moving. She's sitting on the ground, leaning against a wall, not even pulling her legs or arms in to herself. I pound on the ice until pain rattles up past my elbows to my shoulders. I shout at her and then at anyone else, but no one hears and no one comes. I want Mother. I want Mother, but the worst thing is that I know she couldn't help. When I was little I believed she could, no matter what had happened. Nothing could ever be *that* wrong, because there was nothing she couldn't put right. All I had to do was ask.

Standing here, out of breath from screaming at my sister to not die, I feel a different kind of cold inside me. The kind that tells me there's no point wanting Mother. There's nothing at all she could do.

I slither down the wall, wanting to thump it, but my arm is slow and won't obey me.

When the prisoners file out of the ice hall to be locked in their cells for the night, I watch as though it isn't me in here anymore. It's some other girl. I stare at the ice. Stone and ice between me and the world outside Tyur'ma.

The last of the prisoners goes into the cellblock. The Peacekeeper locks the door. Farther down, the boys' block is locked too. The torches are lit on the top of the wall, blinking into life one by one, sending a tiny orange glow through my prison of ice.

And then everything is silent. The stars come out. The wolves' howls are distant. All I want to do is close my eyes. So I do.

I panic as I wake up. There's something wrong with my eyes. I rip a mitten off, though it takes me long seconds to remember how to do it and then to make my hands cooperate. I rub my face, pushing away cold crystals that tear into my eyelashes. Hoarfrost has settled on my lashes. There's nothing wrong with my eyes.

My fingernails are tinged blue. I fumble with my mitten forever, trying to pull it back on. It feels as though my body might crack in the middle as I sit, and I wonder why I woke up at all.

Then I see the orange glow out in the grounds. A faint crackle follows. Smoke trails up into the sky.

A figure runs across the white backdrop of the grounds, but I lose track of it somewhere near the store. The orange glow climbs higher, flickering and growing. *Fire*, I think. Am I dreaming? Is it just a wish for heat that makes it seem so real? Maybe I'm having visions now.

I stare at the fire, watching as it snakes higher into the night sky, while idle thoughts flit through my frozen mind. Shouts ring out, and suddenly I'm awake. Peacekeepers are running over the snow. I crawl to where the door of the dome was. The warden herself, a swath of shifting, slipping gray furs through the ice, strides in front of me toward the fire. It is a fire. A building in the grounds is on fire. I spin around, trying to orient myself. The cellblocks are to my right, still dark, but the doors are open and prisoners are streaming out. In the mad rush, I can't tell who any of them are.

The Peacekeepers yell directions, and I see other prisoners from the boys' block handing out buckets. Moving bodies block my view, but I haul myself to my feet with the dawning realization of which building it is that's on fire.

It's our escape route. It's the tower.

CHAPTER 17

Someone smacks into the ice wall next to me, a muffled thump and a brown blur. But I stand staring in horror at the flames. They have to put it out. They have to save the tower.

"Valor!" It's Katia, banging her mittens against the ice. "Are you all right? Valor!"

I tear my gaze away from the fire. "Katia. I'm fine." I'm not. I know I'm not. My thoughts are stuck in mud, my hands and feet are frozen, and our escape route—the only thing I had left—is burning in front of my eyes.

A girl rushes by and half knocks Katia off her feet. Katia steadies herself. "Warden Kirov says I can get you out now. We need everyone to put out the fire."

I scrabble at the block in front of me, but I can no longer remember where the door was. Katia shoves at one of the blocks, then throws herself at it. Nothing happens. She runs off, coming back with a pickax from the mines. All the while, prisoners and Peacekeepers are shouting over the roar of the fire and everyone is running around, flashes of dark against the snow.

"Stand back," Katia yells, swinging the pickax over her shoulder.

"*No*. Get Sasha first." I press myself to the ice wall. Sasha hasn't moved.

Feliks runs up with a shovel. Katia gestures at him, saying something too low for me to hear. He nods and runs to Sasha's dome, swinging the shovel and driving it into the ice. Katia heaves her pickax forward and it crunches on contact, knocking her off into the snow. She grabs the handle and wrenches.

She swings again and again, each time the momentum of the pickax throwing her body off balance. But she keeps coming back until there's a chink of clear space, air blowing through it. I suck it in gratefully, though it's freezing and acrid with smoke.

Katia pulls at the block, working her hands into the gap, grunting with the effort, until it falls away, hitting the snow with a thunk. And then we both fall on the rest of the blocks, pushing and pulling and hacking them out of the way with the pickax until I fall through the gap, Katia dragging me by the arms.

She clings to me, her face pink, her great, heaving breaths pushing icy clouds into the air. Her arms are limp and shaking as she hugs me. I press Katia tight for a second, then I have to get to Sasha. I stagger upright and stop. Feliks has already dragged her clear of the ice dome. Around him lie the broken remains of the ice door. And on the ground lies Sasha, her lips and eyelids tinged blue, her skin as ashen as the soot-marked snow around her.

I drop to my knees. Katia brushes Sasha's hair back. "She's so cold."

Feliks puts his hand on her neck. "Valor, her heart—it's not working."

I shake my head. No. This can't be happening.

I'm numb all the way through to my heart.

Footsteps stop behind me. "Get her to the infirmary. Her too." It's Dr. Lenina, her face grim, braid slung over her shoulder. There are two prisoners with her, carrying a piece of canvas strung between two poles. "Come with me." The doctor takes my arm as the two prisoners lift Sasha's body onto the stretcher.

I pull away. "No. I have to put the fire out. I have to— the tower." I can't think straight. Everything's fractured like cracked ice.

She shakes her head, about to argue, and I run. My feet have lost all feeling, sending me stumbling into the snow, but I have to put out the fire. I have to stop it burning before everything is destroyed. It's the wrong thing to focus on. Somewhere in the back of my head, I know that. But I can't face the other thing. Not yet. Not now.

Katia runs alongside me, her boots hitting the snow hard. The ground beneath us is solid, compacted by the chaos of all the prisoners running around. One Peacekeeper has a team of maybe forty boys and girls collecting snow in buckets and piling it up against the laundry.

I grab someone near me. "What are they doing?"

The prisoner shakes my hand off. "They're trying to protect the building closest to the tower. Peacekeeper says we have to stop the fire from spreading." She dashes off in the direction of the store.

Something high up on the tower makes a creaking, groaning sound. Katia bites her lip. She knows exactly what it means for us if we don't stop the flames. Sparks and embers float through the smoke-thick air, landing on our clothes. We push forward into the heat, and my hands start stinging and burning. They're not blue anymore, though. The heat is seeping through me now, making my thoughts faster and sharper.

Prisoners shovel snow, banking it up around the fire, but it's melting as fast as they dig.

"We have to do something," I shout to Katia. It can't all be for nothing.

A hot blast of air blows into my face, and I blink warm grit from my eyes. There are four lines of prisoners passing buckets of snow down the chain and throwing it on the flames. Each time it melts in midair, evaporating with a hiss. They need to work faster.

"Come on," I shout to Katia. We run forward. I look around, blinking against the smoke, searching for something I can use to move the ice. If we transport the ice blocks from the domes and throw them onto the fire all at once, maybe we can douse it.

I grab Katia's hand to keep her close. The fire is raging up inside the tower. The door at the bottom is open and burning, and the whole of the interior is engulfed in thick orange flames, burning so fiercely I can hear them roar. The single window at the top of the tower bursts, sending thick shards of glass flying out. We flinch as one smacks into the snow in front of us.

A grinding noise comes from the tower, and for a second the crenelated turret around the top looks as though it's sinking. In slow motion, the midsection of the building crumples, and a wave of heat blasts out.

"Fall back," shouts a Peacekeeper as the first stones tumble and the broken tower looms over us. Prisoners scatter, pushing into one another as they scramble away. Katia's hand is torn from mine, and I'm knocked forward onto the ground. Someone steps on my fingers and I scream, choking on smoke and ash.

I will not lose Katia like this. I will not.

I push up and scan the sooty faces running around me.

"Valor. Valor!" Katia is fighting her way back to me, buffeted on both sides by prisoners slipping on the mud-slush ground. Smoke billows over me, hot and stinking, stinging my eyes and blocking my view.

A hand latches onto my arm. Katia. "Run," she yells, pulling me back toward open ground. So I do. My boots slip. I lose and regain my footing. My lungs feel like they've been roasted, my eyes burn, tears fall down my cheeks. I run.

Around us a rabble of other prisoners run too, until the building behind gives one more crack and hits the ground, sending a shudder through the earth. Smoke and dust roll along the snow and overtake us so we're all running blind, but Katia never lets go of my arm until we're clear on the other side of the prison compound, near the entrance to the mines.

I drop to the ground, coughing and panting. Katia huddles next to me. "Are you hurt?"

I shake my head, though I hardly know whether it's true. My hands and feet feel as though they're on fire. My chest is wheezing, and my throat is raw. Groups of prisoners huddle on the ground around us. Some are running around looking for friends. Some are carrying stretchers, empty or in use, to the infirmary.

Peacekeepers are dotted around the grounds watching the prisoners, but most eyes are still on the blaze. Including Warden Kirov's. She stands by the entrance to the girls' cellblock, a grim look on her face as she watches the ruins of the tower burn.

Nicolai runs toward us, drawing my attention away from the fire. He's frightened. More frightened than any of the other prisoners I've seen tonight looming out of the dark or lit by the flames. Soot smudges one of his eyebrows.

"Are you all right?" he asks. "Do you know if anyone was in the tower?"

"We're fine," says Katia, her hand clasping my arm again.

"Who would have been in the tower?" I ask, but the answer comes to me before I finish the question. Warden Kirov is right here, and the only other person who uses the tower is Prince Anatol.

Nicolai bites his lip. "What about Sasha?"

I can't answer him. I look back to the burning rubble. Dirty snow merges with churned-up mud littered with stones and charred debris. Ash and burning scraps of paper float like dark fairies on the air.

I sit and put my head against Katia's and watch as the tower and the inner wall of Tyur'ma burn. As the ruins go up in smoke, they take with them any hope of us ever escaping from this prison of ice and snow.

CHAPTER 18

It starts snowing in thick sheets. I squint, blinking fat flakes away. There's a strange void around the fire where the snow is falling and melting, but the fire isn't spreading. It's dying down, by inches at first, and then faster. The warden sees it too. She strides in front of us, the smoke at her back smothered by the flurry. Most prisoners are sitting now, clumped together, covered in soot and grime.

"You will be confined to the cellblocks until we have investigated," the warden calls across the grounds.

I suddenly remember the figure I saw running from the tower when I was in the ice dome, before anyone else even noticed the flames. This was no accident. Someone started the fire.

"There will be no work detail tomorrow. Those of you needed for the cleanup and repair operation will be called in the morning and in the following days."

The Peacekeepers start moving among us, forming groups, then lines of prisoners to take back to the cellblocks.

"This one needs to go to the infirmary," says the Peacekeeper standing over me. I hadn't even noticed his arrival. A pair of girls carrying one of Dr. Lenina's stretchers stand next to him, stamping their feet, soot streaking their faces.

I force myself to sit up straight, trying to think of some way to say I can't go without being defiant. I don't want to go in there. Don't want to face what I'll have to face if I do.

Katia puts her arms around me. "Go," she says quietly. "You should go." She jumps up and joins a line heading back to the cellblock before I can even answer. The girls with the stretcher are staring at me.

"I can walk," I say, scrambling to my feet.

Through the snow I see Warden Kirov give the Peacekeeper a nod. I get a long, stone-faced look before another Peacekeeper takes her attention. She's not finished with me.

My Peacekeeper takes my arm and marches me to the infirmary. I try not to drag behind and annoy him, but I'd do anything not to go. I can't bear to see Sasha still in there. I don't know what I'll do. I stumble, half-blinded by the falling snow, toward the infirmary. The Peacekeeper hauls me upright, but I'm crying so suddenly and so hard that it's a miracle I'm still on my feet.

I'm totally disoriented when we reach the doors. He unlocks them, pushes me inside, and locks them again. I stand on the mat crying. Oil lamps are lit in little alcoves all along the walls, and all six beds in the ward are full this time. Dr. Lenina is leaning over one of the beds, directing a girl standing opposite. The doctor glances my way, presses a bowl into the girl's hands, and hurries over to me.

"Valor. Let's put you in here." She moves toward the room I was in last time. I don't follow. The girl lying under the heaped blankets on the bed she was standing by is Sasha.

"I thought she was— I thought—" I break off, sobbing. My legs buckle, and I lean back against the door.

"You know that girl?" Dr. Lenina searches my face, her eyes as kind and concerned as before. I sob harder. I can't meet the doctor's eyes when I choke out, "She's my sister." More than that. She's more myself than I am.

The doctor starts saying something, but I'm hobbling over to Sasha's bedside. She follows me and adjusts the heap of furs that covers Sasha right up to her chin. A tear drips off my jaw onto the bed. I wipe it away, and my fingers creep up to brush Sasha's cheek.

"She's so cold." A spiderweb of tiny blue veins runs across her eyelids.

Dr. Lenina presses her lips together. "She hasn't woken up yet. We just have to keep her warm and hope."

"Is there anything I can do?"

She smiles. "The best thing you can do for your sister is to let me treat you. You don't want to be ill in bed if—*when* she wakes up, do you?"

I shake my head and let her lead me to the room where she treated me before. She makes me take off my boots and coat, gives me clean clothes, and then rebandages my hands. The noise of the ward fades as I sit on the bed, and when the doctor is called away, I slump onto the fresh, white sheets. My hope is burned to the ground, and my heart is ash.

When I wake up, it's still dark. The ward is silent. I slip off the bed and find my furs and boots next to it in a neat pile. Someone has cleaned and dried them. How long have I been asleep? I drink huge gulps of water from the sink, wiping my mouth on the back of my bandages. The sky above the high windows in the infirmary is deep blue, filled with tiny pinpricks of light. There are a couple of oil lamps still burning in the ward, but the room is dim.

Only four of the beds are in use now. Three boys and a girl lie in them, their sleep-heavy breathing the only sound. I pad over to Sasha's bed. Her face is so still. I put my cheek under her nose to check that she's breathing and stay there for some minutes, praying that she keeps on breathing.

"Go back to bed, Valor. There's nothing you can do now." I jump at the sound of Dr. Lenina's voice and spin around to face her. I nod, mute and sad and aching all over, and do what she says.

When I wake again, the door to my room is closed. I blink, knowing that something made me wake, but I don't know what. I flex my fingers. They feel sore, but better. My stomach growls.

"I still need to speak with her. The matter of her interrogation and punishment is still outstanding."

I tense. It's Warden Kirov, and she's right outside the door.

"I understand," says Dr. Lenina in a clipped tone. "But she hasn't regained consciousness yet. And neither has her sister. You can see for yourself."

"I *would* like to see for myself," says the warden, and she swings the door open. The draft it creates ruffles my unbraided hair, but I keep my eyes shut and force my breathing into an even pattern.

"When do you expect her to wake up?" the warden asks, making no attempt to keep her voice down.

"It's impossible to tell with either of them," says the doctor smoothly. "The princess herself has sent an inquiry about the same thing. I can only tell you what I told her. The girls will wake up if and when their bodies allow it. And when they are well enough, I will release them into the cellblocks."

There's a pause. "You told Princess Anastasia that?"

"I told Princess Anastasia *exactly* that," says Dr. Lenina. "As I'm sure you know, I'm bound by oath to safeguard these prisoners and report to our current and future queens, just as you are. She was most concerned about both the possibility that the prince could have been in the tower when the fire started and the welfare of Valor and her sister. It seems she's taking a very personal interest."

The doctor sounds so innocent as she says this that I'm dying to open my eyes a crack to see the look on the warden's face. I don't know if the doctor can stop the warden from punishing me again, but warmth floods through me to think that she would try.

"Yes, it was a blessing that His Royal Highness wasn't present. I shall look forward to having the girls back under my care in the cellblock as soon as possible."

I almost shiver at the warden's icy tone. So the prince wasn't hurt. I'm surprised that I feel relief.

Footsteps sound, and the door clicks shut.

"You can stop pretending now, Valor," says Dr. Lenina.

I open one eye. "You knew I was awake?"

She smiles. "Well, I am a doctor."

I slide my legs over the side of the bed and sit up.

Her smile fades. "Valor, I can't protect you in the cellblock. That's the warden's territory, and I have no power out there."

I swallow. "I know. Thank you for what you've done for me. And for Sasha."

"Thank me by staying here for now," she says. "Eat something. Sit with your sister."

⁓ ✑ ⁓

The next day, I step out of the infirmary, blinking in the dazzling brightness of the grounds. Peacekeeper Rurik has been sent to fetch me, and I have no choice but to leave Sasha in Dr. Lenina's care. I feel it, though—like an invisible thread running between the two of us is pulled tight when I walk out of the building and into the snow.

A group of thirty or so prisoners is working on the site where the tower stood. The inner wall is half rebuilt already. Warden Kirov must have had teams working day and night. The rubble has been carted away, and the uneven ground is covered in a thick blanket of snow.

It's as though the tower was never there. The tunnel is buried under the stone, which has sunk into the lower level. I turn away. I wanted to stay with Sasha, but how can I tell her that we'll both spend the rest of our lives in prison? Another grim thought pushes into my head—that the rest of our lives might not even be a very long time. I can't hold Warden Kirov or Prince Anatol at bay with the threat of Princess Anastasia forever. And what use will her royal mercy be if we're both dead?

Peacekeeper Rurik unlocks the cellblock door and barely waits for me to enter before locking it again. Below me, long tables like those in the ice hall have been set up. All the cell doors are rolled open, and the girls who aren't working are gathered in various spots around the building.

"Valor!" Katia rushes over. "Are you okay? Is Sasha? What happened?"

I take her hand, trying to think of a few words of explanation. Over her shoulder, I see Natalia, who was sitting at one of the tables but is now making her way toward us.

I pull Katia forward and rush up the steps to our cell. I throw myself on my bunk, facing the wall.

Footsteps follow us. "What's the matter, Valor? That's no way to greet your sister's new cellmate."

I scramble up on the bed. Katia twists her hands together.

"Since when?" I ask.

"Since yesterday," says Natalia. "But don't worry—we're going to get along just fine. I'll look after her when she gets out of the infirmary. Back to more important things. Do you have a new plan?" She's leaning on the rolled-back door of my cell with her arms folded. Her ankles are crossed, the toe of her boot resting on the smooth stone of the floor.

I don't answer. This is worse than when Sasha was with the Black Hands. At least she was in a solitary cell up there. Not even my sister can charm Natalia.

Natalia leans forward. "No new plan? Well, you'd better make one."

"We're not going *anywhere* without Sasha." As soon as I say it, I realize I'm not defeated. I'm not going to let Natalia know how it will eat at me to know she's in a cell at night with my sister. I'm not going to tell Sasha she'll never get out of here. I can't do that to her, or to the others. Feliks and Katia are my friends. And I can't let everything they've done to help me be for nothing. Katia sits on the bed and puts her arm around me.

"I'll find another way, I promise," I say to Natalia. "But I'm not going anywhere without Sasha."

On the third day of our confinement in the cellblock, Warden Kirov announces that the wall is rebuilt and work detail will start again the next day. Every time a Peacekeeper has entered the cellblock in the last two days, I've been worried, expecting Warden Kirov to have sent for me. But she hasn't yet.

We're taken to the ice hall for breakfast. We work in the mines and eat our evening meal in the ice hall again, and I go back to my cell tired and worried about Sasha coming back and finding she's stuck with Natalia as a cellmate.

As the Peacekeeper calls for us to step into the cellblock on the sixth day, I have to shove my hand over my mouth to keep from crying out in surprise. There, already inside, is Sasha. I fill to the brim with emotion, like the bubbling wine that fills Mother's glass on her birthday.

She smiles and steps forward awkwardly. I run in, pushing past the other girls filing toward their cells, and throw my arms around her. We hug each other tight.

"I'm sorry, I'm so sorry." The words burst out of me. They're all I've been thinking and feeling for days.

She pries my arms off her neck, laughing quietly. "I'm all right. Listen, Natalia already saw me on her way past. She said we don't need to wait any longer. Do you know what she meant?"

I keep hold of Sasha's hands, not willing to let her go.

"It means she's been waiting for me to come up with another plan, and now that you're here . . ."

"We don't need to wait any longer." Sasha's eyes take on a fierce look. "Do you really still mean for us to escape?" She takes my hands and gently turns them over. They're still pink and sore.

"Only if you want to. I can't risk you again. You almost—" I can't even say it.

She flicks my forehead like Katia did, right between my eyebrows.

"Fine," I say. "I'll take it that you do."

Two days later, Nicolai calls out the work detail as we stand behind our places in the ice hall. Despite the fact that we scrubbed the entire kitchen and everything in it yesterday, Feliks still has a dirty mark on his neck. Katia frowns at it as Nicolai says that we're working in the laundry today. He's been quiet since the day I saw him in the prison grounds after the tower crumbled. Today is no different. He directs us to our workstations in the laundry, giving himself and two other boys the job of collecting the mountains of dirty clothes and bringing them to us at the tubs. The Peace-keeper guarding us takes up a position at the door as usual.

The room to the left, where the laundry is gathered, is full almost to the ceiling. Warden Kirov halted all nonessen-tial work until the repairs were complete (although Katia has muttered on several occasions that cleaning clothes is not what she considers nonessential), and we're going to have to work hard today to clear the pile.

Natalia gives me a look as she takes off her coat. She watches me constantly, and I know she's going to lose patience soon. She doesn't need to tell me that Sasha will pay for it if she does; I can think of nothing else. Maybe she's lost patience now, because she strides across the room and gets right up close to me. "Warden Kirov is going to sum-mon Sasha before evening meal tonight."

I stiffen. "How do you know that?"

Natalia shrugs, a smirk breaking out on her face. "I know people. I hear things."

"What does she want with Sasha?"

"What do you think? She tried questioning you about what went on the night you got out of the cellblock. She tried punishing your sister. Now she's going to drag it out of her." She shrugs again. "Just thought you should know."

She saunters off back to her workstation. I kneel at a tub, scrubbing garments with my hands plunged up to the elbows in soapy water. It's just my body going through the motions, though. All I can think of is the numbness and the terror I felt when I thought I'd lost Sasha.

Sweat soon mixes with the steam condensing on my brow. Despite Dr. Lenina's miracle salve, my hands are still sore.

"What did Natalia want?" asks Katia.

"Nothing," I say. "Just the usual." Natalia's trying to force me into getting her out of here. It might all be a lie about Sasha. Still, I can't stop thinking about it as I scrub.

After a while, Katia sighs. "This is making the clothes dirtier than they were before. We need clean water."

"Nicolai!" I call to him as he carries another armful of trousers and undergarments to Sasha and Feliks, who are working on the same side of the room as we are.

He stops, trailing a grubby tunic on the floor.

"We need to change the water." I rattle the chain anchoring the tub in place. Water slops over the side and trickles under the tub, and ideas slot into place in my head like arrows hitting a target one after another: we're not usually allowed to change the water. It doesn't normally need to be done, but there's more laundry than usual today. The water must drain away to somewhere. The drains must run under the prison, like the tunnels. And they must lead somewhere—probably to the water plant outside the city.

"Valor?" Nicolai frowns at me. And, of course, Natalia has noticed. Nothing gets past her.

"I— We just need clean water," I say. But it's not like the Peacekeeper is going to hand me a set of keys to unlock the tubs. Nicolai chews his cheek. He's thinking the same thing.

"I'll ask," he says.

Before he's even made it to the Peacekeeper stationed at the door, Natalia is by my side. "I saw that look on your face. What is it?" She's already looking around, trying to figure out what's going on. "Maybe you need a reminder of who I share a cell with now. Maybe Sasha will have an accident tonight."

I clench my fingers around the rim of the tub, digging my nails into the wood. "I'm working on something. There might be drains below."

A glint comes into her eyes. "*Might* be?"

Nicolai walks back across the room, giving me the barest shake of his head. But we need those keys. These tubs can't be moved unless we can unlock the chains. I have no way of seeing the drains underneath the prison without them.

"Okay, there *are* drains," I tell Natalia. "But I need to see them first. And you have to give me time to think about how we're going to do this."

She gives me a long, hard look and then walks away. We all get on with our work, but my thoughts are flitting around the whole time. Can I risk asking Feliks to steal another set of keys? When do they empty the water out of the tubs—after we're finished for the day? I only register that Natalia has called for the Peacekeeper at her workstation when Katia nudges me. I keep my eyes lowered and my hands busy as he walks past. Seconds later there's a muffled grunt and a weight hitting the floor.

I spin around. Natalia is standing over the Peacekeeper, who's crumpled unconscious next to her washtub. She has an iron bucket in her hand.

"Don't say I never do anything for you, Valor," she says.

Sasha's wide eyes meet mine from across the room. "What have you done?" she asks Natalia in a cracked whisper.

For a few seconds we all freeze, no one moving, no one speaking.

But as I'm staring at the Peacekeeper, horrified, that's when I know there's no going back now.

"What are you waiting for?" asks Natalia. "Get the keys. Let's go."

"Valor?" Nicolai's hands are clenched at his sides.

I shake my head at him and then dart forward and detach the keys from the Peacekeeper's belt. He's breathing. I don't know how long we have before he wakes up.

"Valor, what about them?" Feliks's voice is urgent. He points up the stairs in the middle of the room. The two boys who have been helping Nicolai are on the upper level of the laundry putting endless garments on rows of lines to dry.

"We'll just have to give them something that keeps them busy for a while," says Sasha, her gaze already on the other tubs full of sopping-wet clothes.

I give one sharp nod at her, and then slot the keys into the locks on the chains until I find the right one. I have to force myself not to keep looking at the Peacekeeper, not to think about what Warden Kirov will do to us if we don't make this work.

Katia's face is twisted in determination. She searches my eyes, and we get to work in grim silence, pulling at the chains, unspooling them from the anchors on the tub.

The chains snake loose across the floor. I take up a stance by the tub and put my weight behind it to tip out the dirty water, but it doesn't budge. Feliks joins me, then Katia, and eventually it tilts, and dirty water starts to slosh over the side. Once the water starts pouring, it's easy to keep it coming in a cascade.

Nicolai hovers at my elbow, casting frantic glances at the door and at the Peacekeeper still prone on the floor. "You need to stop, Valor. This is—"

"I know. I didn't exactly ask Natalia to do that, did I? But what happens if we stop now?"

He doesn't have an answer.

Sasha and Feliks drag all the sopping-wet clothes they can carry from the tubs and shove them through the presses that squeeze out the water. They run relays of the piles upstairs until I hear complaints from the two boys.

"That should keep them busy for a while," says Sasha. She's out of breath just like the rest of us, her arms shining with water and soap suds. Her eyes are shining too, wild and hectic, anxious but hopeful, and her face is flushed, just as I imagined her when I walked down the tunnel on the night I went to the tower. It calms my nerves and steels my resolve.

Feliks nudges me with his elbow. He's looking at Natalia. She's almost grinning in satisfaction. I run around to the other side of the tub where she's standing and watch the water stream down a drain with an iron grille over it. A round grille just big enough for a small person to fit through.

I reach down as the last of the water gurgles away, leaving a soapy scum on the bars. My fingers hook the iron, and my heart pounds in my ears as I pull. The grille lifts away in my hand, and I almost fall backward.

Natalia claps me on the shoulder like we're friends. "I knew you could do it, Valor."

Nicolai wipes his shaking hands down his trousers. His eyes flit around the group and then return to me. "Are you seriously thinking of doing this *now*?"

I look at him. I don't know what I'm thinking anymore. Little stabbing nerves pinch at my stomach.

My sister takes my arm. "Valor, this is no less dangerous than your first plan. Getting caught means exactly the same thing no matter how or when we go."

"She couldn't be more right," says Natalia.

"I know," I snap at her.

And what choice do we have after what Natalia did to the Peacekeeper? But this pipe has to come out somewhere, and there's no time to find out more, no time to trust or not trust. There's only now and a chance to go. I look around the team. Each of them looks back, and I know it's time to get them out of here. "Can you run?" I ask Sasha.

She nods.

I nod back. "Let's go."

Natalia turns to Nicolai. "Are you with us or against us?"

"I'm with you," he says to her, but he's looking at me.

"Let's not waste any more time, then," I say.

We all pull our furs on. I hope we won't have to ditch them anywhere. We won't survive outside for long without them.

I pull the grille fully clear of the drain and get down on my stomach. The opening drops away into darkness, but I can see white suds floating about six or seven feet below. They trail off along another pipe. It will be a tight fit for us—especially for Natalia—but it's just big enough. I don't know where the pipe goes, though, and I have a moment of fresh doubt.

"Happy to go first," says Natalia, pulling my shoulder and rolling me out of the way. She sits at the edge of the open drain and then drops away into the pipe with no hesitation. Feliks scrambles after her. He drops to the bottom and lifts his face to peer back up at us, then disappears into the pipe. Katia goes next, fear widening her eyes as she falls.

"You next," I say to Nicolai. I want to get Sasha out of here so badly that it's almost a physical need, like being thirsty. But I want him in front of us. Between his cautious nature and the way he's struggling now, he might panic and give us away if I leave him behind.

He chews on his lip and then disappears silently down the pipe.

"Now you." Sasha nods, and suddenly crushes me in a hug that almost knocks me over.

I squeeze her back, then pull her arms from around me. "We have to go."

She drops, and I sit at the edge of the drain myself. I take a deep breath and follow her, my stomach flipping.

The wall of the drain, slick with water and slime, flashes past, and I land with a bone-jarring thud at the bottom. The pipe in front of me is small and dark. All I can see are the soles of Sasha's boots. It smells faintly of the soap we use in the laundry, but mostly of something dank and cold.

"Are you okay?" I whisper. My voice sounds strange in the cramped space.

"I'm fine," she calls back. There's no room for her to turn and look at me.

I don't care if I have to crawl all the way to the city on my hands and knees, as long as this works. Everything inside me tingles, part horror and part hope. I shuffle forward and wish I'd put my mittens on first as my hands sink into inches of sludge in the pipe. Our little convoy crawls forward into the dark, hands and knees sliding through something I don't wish to think about, our breathing loud in the tight space.

My knees start to hurt. Natalia's moving quickly, setting a pace I would be happy with if I couldn't hear Sasha panting with effort.

"Keep going," I say to her. I try not to think of anything but putting my hands one in front of the other. Fear will freeze me if I let myself think about Warden Kirov. However hard I try to keep them out, though, thoughts edge into my head. Peacekeepers are much too big to fit into the pipe. But other prisoners aren't. Prisoners who might be given knives or crossbows. I hold back a shudder in the dark and keep moving.

After a while, I lose all sense of time and direction. My hands and knees are numb, my arms aching, legs cramping. The air is stale and reeks of mold. It feels like we must be in the center of the city by now, right under the palace. But we could just as easily be a mile under the frozen earth with nothing but a wasteland of snow and snarling wolves above us. I can't hear anything but the tiny echo of panted breath.

What seems like hours later, Natalia calls out. It might be my imagination, but it does look lighter ahead. My arms are shaking and my knees are tender. I'm sure they must be bruised black by now.

And then I hear a rushing noise behind us, like wind blowing through trees, or . . . water.

CHAPTER 19

The sound is distant at first, like the sea from the shore, but it grows louder fast. Rusting flakes of iron scratch my arms as I close the gap between Sasha and me. The sound becomes a roar, and the space in the pipe seems to vibrate. Cold sweat breaks out across my skin. My hands and knees scrabble beneath me, but I can't make them go fast enough.

"Valor?" Sasha's voice is raw with panic.

"Hold your breath," I tell her desperately. Someone ahead lets out a sob, and then the roar fills my ears. Katia screams.

Freezing water surges up and covers me in the blackness, drenching my clothes, knocking the breath out of me as it drags me forward into Sasha. The cold is shocking, constricting my chest, stopping every thought before I can form it.

Something hits me hard—a boot, maybe—and I lose whatever air is left in my lungs. I panic, my arms flailing against the tight space of the pipe. I'm going to drown. I've made it this far, and Warden Kirov is going to drown me. We'll be stuck in the pipes forever; no one will know what happened to us. I need air.

I open my mouth, and freezing, scummy water rushes in. Then just as suddenly as it washed over us, the water passes, and I drop in a heap, gasping and coughing. Water floods down my nose, burning, and I cough and cough, heaving air into my lungs in between.

"Sasha? Sasha?"

"I'm okay."

I wipe water from my face, sucking in huge, ragged breaths. "We have to get out of here. Is everyone okay?"

Scared voices answer me. Someone is sobbing. Nicolai coughs so hard it must be painful, and Feliks curses. But we either move, or Warden Kirov pours more water down the drain and we die.

"I think there's a way out ahead," calls Natalia, and even she sounds shaken.

"Then go," I yell back. "Go. Go!"

My chest heaves, and I'm shaking. My clothes are sodden, weighted down and making me slow, but I push myself on. I won't let Sasha down now. Ahead of me, Natalia cries out. Katia calls back, "We made it!" I can hear the relief in her voice, and I crawl faster. Air blows on my face, and then I sense Sasha disappearing from in front of me. Hands reach out and grab my arms, pulling me into a place where I can stand.

"I think we're in the sewage system," says Sasha from somewhere near me.

"I do too," I say. "At least, that's what I was hoping for."

"Are you sure?" asks Katia.

"Well, if we are," says Sasha, "then, logically speaking, there should be . . ." A few scuffling noises come from close by in the dark.

A tiny, bright light flares, and I see Sasha's face, her braids dripping down her chest, before I blink and shield my eyes. She had a fire inch-stick in her fingers. The light changes and I look back, my eyes watering at the sudden brightness. She's holding an oil lamp. The others are standing with expressions ranging from delight to confusion, all of them breathing hard, all soaked and shivering.

"Where did you get that?" asks Feliks.

"There," says Sasha, holding the lamp up behind her. The circle of light shows a shelved alcove in a stone wall just big enough to hold the lamp. "If these are maintenance tunnels, then there have to be workers to maintain them. And workers have to have light, don't they?" There's stunned silence. "Well, any of you could have thought of that," she says.

Feliks and Katia exchange looks, their mouths open in little circles.

"She's right," says Nicolai, shaking water from his hat. "And I know there's a water plant outside the city. Maybe ten miles from here."

Natalia steps forward. "Fascinating as this is, we need to move. Any idea which way we should go?"

Sasha holds her lamp high. The weak glow shows an arched tunnel built of stone, cold and damp, but big enough to walk upright through. Another gush of water blasts out of the pipe, making me jump into Katia. Sasha pushes forward with the lamp, and we watch as the water blasts into the middle of the tunnel and flows away. "We follow that to the water plant," she says.

My teeth are chattering, but I smile. We run in the direction the water flows, our boots echoing in the tunnel.

Along the wall, there are other little alcoves, and at each, Feliks makes it his job to stop and hurriedly light an oil lamp. After a few miles, we have four, including the one I'm holding. We're running close to the wall when something that I recognize flashes past in the dim light. I jolt to a stop. Nicolai, bringing up the rear now, runs into me. "Wait!" I call ahead.

The others turn and gather around.

"What is it?" asks Sasha. She looks tired, dark shadows flickering under her eyes. Worry flashes through me. I wish we could slow or stop to let her rest.

I lift my lamp to where a smaller tunnel with bright mosaic tiles covered in cobwebs leads off to the left. I recognize the patterns—they're the same as those in the tunnels under the tower in Tyur'ma.

"I think this is part of the tunnel I was planning to use before the tower burned. If it is, we can get straight to the city this way."

Finally—*finally* my plan is going to work. "Come on." Cobwebs stick to my face as I tear down the tunnel, everyone following me. My legs burn, but my heart is soaring now. And when I see light ahead, I laugh out loud.

We burst into a tunnel that's obviously been swept clean. A few oil lamps burn on the walls. The light is dim, the oil almost burned down. There are spaces where some of the lamps have gone out altogether.

I look to the left. In the distance a pile of rubble blocks the entire space. It's the cave-in that happened when the tower was destroyed. And it means Warden Kirov can't follow us. I don't even pause to regain my breath. I ditch my lamp and run in the opposite direction, the sound of five pairs of boots following me.

The bright colors of the mosaics fly past. My breath becomes ragged, and my still-wet clothes rub my skin and make me feel like I'm running through mud. But I'm running, and my sister is next to me, her braids flying out behind her, bumping on her back.

I check over my shoulder. Katia is lagging behind, but her head is up, and she has a determined look in her eye.

Feliks is flying along, his thin frame bouncing with every step.

The tunnel branches into four in front of us. I memorized where each one leads from Father's plans. Straight ahead leads to the palace, and right leads to the docks. I hold out an arm to point the direction to the others and turn right. I have to slow down, though, because this tunnel isn't in use and there are no lamps.

I take Sasha's hand. "Make a chain," I say. Natalia's still got her oil lamp, so she leads the way. Sasha links her other hand with Feliks's, and he links with Katia, and we're running again, Nicolai at the back, until I see light—real daylight slanting down in broken shafts as if through bars.

I hold onto Sasha's hand as if it's a life raft. We're going to make it. We're the first people in three hundred years to escape from Tyur'ma.

"Put out your lamp, Natalia," I whisper. "We can't risk being seen now."

She snuffs the flame, and we creep toward the exit of the tunnel above us. Light streams in through the iron grille. The salty tang of sea air blows into my face, but there's something not far above the bars. Slats of wood. Water sloshes nearby. I can't see enough to work out exactly where we are.

"Here." Natalia shuffles through the group and offers me her back to climb up on and see. Hands reach out to steady me as she lifts me to the grille. I wrap my fingers around the bars, frightened for a moment that they won't give. But black flakes prickle my fingers and rain down to the floor of the tunnel. The iron has been corroded by the salt air.

I push up, the weight of the grille sinking onto my arms. Underneath me, Natalia shifts to one side and then rights herself. The whole cover moves, and the grating of it sounds loud in the tunnel. I freeze, holding my breath. Katia has one hand over her mouth, the other clinging to Feliks's shoulder. I ease the bars to one side and peek over the edge. Above me is a dockside building built on small wooden stilts. We'll have to crawl along the ground through the gap to get out. Ahead, though, I see a slice of blue sea beyond stone walls, a collection of boats rocking gently on the water. Closest to us is a group of small fishing boats with nets strewn around the sides, and on the other side of the harbor sits an enormous, elegant sailing ship with towering masts and yards and yards of furled sails.

"Okay, let me down," I say. I'm just about to describe the scene to the others when there's a voice from down the tunnel. A flash flood of panic washes through me. Katia's eyes are wide, her breathing fast.

I point to Sasha. *You first.*

She shakes her head, pushing Feliks in front of her. I open my mouth, but there's a faint noise from somewhere that makes all our heads whip toward it. Nobody moves; everybody's poised, waiting. I take shallow little breaths.

There it is again. No mistaking the source: boots echoing in the tunnels. I lock my fingers together to make a foothold, but Natalia shoves me out of the way and makes her own, her broad back filling half the tunnel. Feliks gives me an anxious look, his eyes big in the dim light, and hops up onto Natalia's hands. She lifts him easily. He scrambles through the gap, and his boots vanish.

Sasha pulls Katia forward next, and I don't argue. A few weeks ago I thought I would have stepped over anyone to get Sasha and Sasha alone out of Tyur'ma. But if I got out and any one of my friends didn't, I know how I'd feel. They are all Sasha now. We help lift Katia up. She struggles for a moment before she's pulled forward from above.

The footfalls get closer, heavy boots echoing on the stone floor. A male voice says something, and another answers. They're so close; everything inside me is screaming to run, run, run.

Natalia offers her locked hands to Sasha. I would love with all of my heart to push my sister up there and leave Natalia. But I look at her and she looks at me, and just for a second I see that she's realized she might not be able to get up there without help. She's heavy, and the tunnel grille is high.

I offer her my hands. She blinks twice, then puts her boot into them and steps up. I'm almost knocked down, but the voices at my back make me strong with desperation. I heave as hard as I can, Sasha helping, and Natalia grabs the lip of the opening and slowly, agonizingly, pulls herself up.

Out of the gloom behind us, men dressed in black appear. One of them shouts, and they all run straight at us. I turn around, but Nicolai has vanished. Where did he go? When did he leave? I don't have time to think about the sting I feel.

"Move," I scream at Sasha. She shoves her boot into my hands, and I barely feel her weight. I fling her up at the hole, and she clings to it and climbs out. She made it. I jump higher than I have ever jumped before, and my fingers grasp the edge on the first try. Sasha grabs my wrists, her face frantic above mine, and I'm going to make it. I'm going to make it too.

An arm wraps around my waist. I kick out and pull up. But whoever has hold of me is a dead weight dragging me to the ground. My fingers slip. I drop down into the tunnel.

"Run," I shout before I even look to see who holds me. "Run, Sasha, run!"

"You can't help her now. Come with me," I hear Natalia say from above. It sounds like there's genuine desperation in her voice.

I struggle against the grip on me, but my arms are pinned by my side now.

Sasha's face appears above, twisted in anguish. "I can't go without you, Valor."

"Run, Sasha! Get away!"

I hear Natalia above us. "Come with me, Sasha!"

Sasha's chin juts. "I won't leave without you." Her face disappears and I pray she ran, even if it's with Natalia, but then her boots come into view. As she drops back down into the tunnel next to me, I sag against the arms that are locked around me, hurting my waist.

"Take them both," says the person holding me. "You know where to put them. I have to go."

I stiffen and buck against him. I know that voice. It's Prince Anatol.

"Come on, Nicolai," he says.

I wrench my way out of his grip and swing around to face the prince. "You're a thief and a liar," I yell. "You can't do this to us." I turn on Nicolai, my face flaming, anger raging. "And you, you traitor. You're working for *him*. You sneaked off to inform on us? To bring him here? I hate you. I hate you both! I—"

"We don't have time for this," the prince cuts in. He turns to one of the men in black. The blue sashes on their uniforms match his tunic. His own personal guards. "Take them. Keep them quiet. I'll deal with this later."

Two guards grab me.

I kick and scream until one of the guards shoves something in my mouth and ties a gag around the back of my head, and then I slump to the floor and refuse to walk at all until one of them takes hold of Sasha's arm and drags her in front of me. After that I sink into a sullen silence as they bind our hands and lead us back the way we came.

There are four guards, two on either side of us. They make Sasha walk behind me so I can't even see her. We walk back to the where the tunnels branch, and they march us down the one that leads to the palace. All I can think about is how close we were. I tasted the sea air. I felt the breeze rolling in from the harbor. And now the prince has won, thanks to that traitor, Nicolai.

Eventually we reach a grille that I wouldn't have noticed if we weren't yanked to a halt beneath it. There's no light coming from above. I try not to think about where the prince could want us held, or what he meant when he said he'd deal with us later. My throat keeps pushing against the gag in my mouth. I wish I hadn't screamed so loud before. I might need to again before long.

When the guard next to me moves, I see a rope ladder hooked onto the grille. A guard pushes the bars aside and climbs up. Another unties our hands. I think about making a run for it, but Sasha's guards are still blocking her in on both sides. Instead I'm prodded up the ladder, my feet swinging out awkwardly below me as I climb out into a strange jungle.

The air is hot and somehow wet at the same time. All around us are lush, green leaves and big frilled orange flowers. Thick perfume hangs on the heavy air. Vines cascade down, dripping with flowers so bright a shade of pink that I don't believe they're real.

Sasha climbs up to stand next to me. I follow her gaze up to the ceiling. High above us, a domed glass ceiling arches within a delicate silver frame, the sky beyond it a frosty white. We're in the palace hothouse.

My clothes drip onto the path as the guards march us to a small door at the back. It leads to a darkened hall that turns into a maze of cold, windowless corridors. I try to keep my bearings, but we're hurried along, my guards yanking me forward. One of them stops at an intersection, but instead of turning left or right, he slides open a panel in the wall in front of us.

I try to catch a glimpse of Sasha, but the guards march us through the opening into a dark wood-paneled room and then through another hidden door into a colder wing of the palace, where the lamps aren't lit and the only light comes from the sliver of window showing through the heavy drapery. There's dust in the air.

My shoulders tighten. I have no idea where we're being taken, or why. Without warning, halfway down a dim corridor, one of the guards opens a door, casts us both into a room, and closes the door again.

I rush forward to grab the heavy wooden handle, only to hear it lock from the outside. I rip the gag away, spitting the balled-up material in my mouth onto a rug on the floor. It's a wolf pelt, thick and silvery and tinged with white on the tips. It covers most of the dark wood floor that isn't taken up by a high four-poster bed.

I turn to Sasha only to see her confused expression mirroring my own. Thick crimson drapes are tied back with golden ropes at each post on the bed. There's a matching crimson-and-gold coverlet. It looks soft and thick.

Over against the window stands a dark wood dresser with a china basin and a gilded mirror on top of it. Two faces with wild, messy braids and bedraggled furs stare back at me. I run over to the window and look down. A sheer drop of two floors leads to a sunken garden, frozen with snow that glitters in the dying sun. I wrench at the frame and then the glass itself, but nothing gives. I search the dresser—the only piece of furniture in the room—for anything that could help us escape, but it contains only a few items of clothing and a silver hairbrush. Sasha finds an ornate headdress inlaid with pearls. I can only imagine how much it's worth. Little use to us now.

I scan the rest of the room. There's another door. Sasha spots it at the same time I do, and we both run for it. It's unlocked. Hope bursts up like a fountain. I swing the door wide, and it opens into a marble bathing room with a sunken bath. There are no doors or windows.

"I . . . don't understand," says Sasha. "I don't know why we're here." She shivers, and I remember we're still soaked from the water in the pipe.

"I don't know either," I say, though I'm trying hard not to think of how unused this wing of the palace seems. We could be locked in here for days, and no one would know. Maybe the prince isn't as hands-on with his punishments as Warden Kirov. I don't want Sasha to think about that, though.

Still, something isn't right. Something doesn't make sense, and it's gnawing at me the same way hunger did that first day in Tyur'ma.

For long minutes, we search every part of the room—under the bed, behind the dresser, fingers prying at the panels on the walls. Eventually we stop, wet, tired, and cold.

"Valor?" Sasha eyes the bath. "I'm so cold. Even if we could escape, we'd freeze."

She's right. We need to be warm and dry or we'll never make it. And who knows what damage this is doing to my sister, with her already weakened by the warden's ice dome?

I step forward onto the marble floor. Soon we're both shedding our damp clothes and running water into the bath. I'm not about to let my sister freeze when she doesn't have to.

When we're both clean and dry, we put on the clothes from the dresser—a couple of tunics that are finer than anything that's touched my skin in my entire life. Sasha's is too big, but it doesn't matter. Her eyes are unfocused, and she's blinking slowly, exhausted. She sits on the bed to brush out her tangle of hair. The covers are as soft as they look, and she sinks into them. I sit behind her and start at the bottom of my own hair, teasing out one knot at a time.

"Do you think the others got away?" I ask.

"I think so. Natalia was the only one still there when I climbed up." Sasha looks over her shoulder and frowns. "You know, she didn't seem very concerned with getting away at first. In fact, she was waiting for us. Natalia wanted me to go with her."

"Are you sure?" I ask, but I remember the sound of Natalia's voice. She *did* try to make Sasha go with her. And she helped everybody else get out instead of putting herself first. Something else that doesn't make sense. She cared nothing for Sasha. And I've never met anyone who cared more about herself than Natalia. Why wouldn't she run as fast and as far away as she could? I open my mouth to give some kind of explanation, but I can't think of anything.

Sasha's head nods forward, and she sways. She leans back onto the bed and curls up like a mouse, already asleep. I know how she feels. All my muscles ache, and the bed is so soft. I'm warm from the hot bath, so warm that it's like medicine making me drowsy. I haven't been properly warm, all the way through my body, in weeks. And even though I'm scared and have no idea what's going on, I can barely keep my eyes open. I need to think. I'm missing something important, I know it.

I wake with a start, moonlight falling through the window and across the bed. A key turns in the lock. I scuttle backward until I hit the headboard. The door opens, and I shake Sasha awake. A figure steps into the room. The light glints on the gold fist clasped at his throat.

Prince Anatol.

CHAPTER 20

I keep still and wait to see how many guards are with him, my heart suddenly pounding so hard it makes me dizzy. He steps fully into the room, holding an oil lamp in one hand and closing the door with the other. Alone.

I feel around for something to clock him over the head with, but he holds up a hand. "Don't bother. I had the room searched thoroughly before you were brought here, and unless you plan to smother me to death, I'm afraid you'll just have to listen. I'm sorry for your treatment yesterday, but there wasn't time to explain, and you insisted on all that screaming and kicking."

I pull myself up straight and scramble out on top of the covers. "I—what?"

Sasha rubs her face. "Valor?"

"And Prince Anatol," I say in a hard voice.

She bolts upright, eyes wide, her hair massed around her head like a messy halo. "What's going on?"

"His Highness has come to chide me for kicking and screaming when he had his guards gag me and drag us to the palace to lock us up for a crime he knows you didn't commit." I hold my head high, more angry than scared now.

He gives a long, drawn-out sigh. "If you hadn't made that ridiculous escape, I wouldn't have had to put you in here. You made me do it."

I shake my head. "What are you talking about? We didn't make you do anything."

He crosses the room and puts the lamp on the dresser. "Why do you think you're here instead of in the dungeon? Or back in Tyur'ma?" Prince Anatol rubs his hands over his face. "I'm on your side."

I jump off the bed and face him. My heart is beating fast, but I've known something wasn't right since we were brought here. I glance at my sister. She knows it too. That doesn't mean I'm going to trust him just like that, just because he says so.

"You stopped us from escaping," I say. "Do you really expect us to think you could possibly be on our side?"

"I expect you to realize I always was," he says. "You really are a completely bull-headed girl."

"And you are arrogant and self-serving and—and—*sneaky*."

"Don't you remember when I told Dr. Lenina to help you after you burned your hands?"

"Yes, but—"

"Don't you remember when I had Sasha released from the Black Hands so you could be together? I couldn't prove Sasha was innocent, but I could at least do that."

I take a step back. Sasha sits up straighter.

"But that was Princess Anastasia," I say.

"And what about Nicolai?" asks Sasha. "He betrayed us. He's working for you." My sister's eyes are narrowed slightly, trained on the prince. She's testing him, digging for information.

The moonlight hits the prince's hair from the back, making the tips of his curls silver. "Yes, he's working for me. He was *supposed* to watch over you, not let you escape. I was going to have you released after I found out who stole the music box." He frowns. "I've questioned every member of the staff. But then you had to go and escape before I could discover anything at all."

He pulls an envelope out of his tunic and offers it to me.

"I brought you something," he says in a low voice. "Something to make you believe me."

I take the letter from him. "What is this?"

"Warden Kirov returned it to me after she took it from you," he says. "She didn't open it, since I hadn't given it to her personally. The royal seal is untouched still."

Sasha and I exchange a glance. We wait for him to speak further, but abruptly he crosses the room, takes up the lamp, and leaves. I rush to the door, only to hear the lock click. Of all the strange things that have happened over the last few weeks, this may be the strangest. I half expect to wake up in the morning and find that I've been dreaming.

Sasha steps closer. "Open it, then, Valor."

I turn the letter over. It's a little crumpled, but it's the same one that I took from the tower, that dropped from my furs in the forge. I break the seal and scan the contents with my sister. It covers one brief page, written in a sloping hand.

Warden Kirov,

Forgive the shortness and incompleteness of this letter. I am writing with information of a highly sensitive nature, and as yet have only the scantest of intelligence upon which to base it. I have reason to believe that inmate Sasha Raisayevna is innocent.

I lose focus trying to absorb the last sentence. There are a few other details, but nothing substantial. Nothing that proves Sasha's innocence or even suggests who the real culprit is. There's a snowstorm in my head, tiny bits of doubt and disbelief whirling together.

I read the words at the end:

I commend my findings so far to your care and discretion, and charge you with conveying this information to my mother, Queen Ana, in the event that any mishap should befall me.

The truth floats into my head like a lone snowflake. The snowflake rolls down a hill, gathering speed and more snow. "It's someone else. Someone in the palace. It's not Anatol at all." Saying it out loud brings it into focus.

Sasha's eyes are huge. "He said he questioned all the staff."

My sister and I look at each other. Because if it wasn't Anatol, and he hasn't been able to find out who it was, it's because he's been looking in the wrong places. There *is* an explanation, but it's one he wouldn't want to see.

Sasha's thinking the same thing. And she looks crushed. I put my arm around her. How could the princess do this to her? *Why?*

"But why would Anastasia steal it?" I ask.

Sasha drops to the bed. She's breathing fast, her face scrunched in concentration. "I think—I think maybe Anastasia has made an alliance with Pyots'k, behind Queen Ana's back."

"What?" I shake my head. "But Queen Ana wants peace with Magadanskya, with Lady Olegevna."

My sister nods. "She does. But Anastasia is almost thirteen now. She'll soon be queen herself. Think about it. Why else would she do it?

"Queen Ana chose her allies for the good of the realm—to lessen the possibility of war, to strengthen Demidova against Pyots'k and their incessant requests to use our ports. But I think Anastasia doesn't care why they want to use them. Remember I told you how many questions she asked about it? I thought she was interested in the politics. I thought she was learning. But maybe she kept asking because she couldn't see that the riches they offered in return aren't worth involving us in the war Pyots'k wants to wage."

It surprises me—not that Sasha can get to the heart of why Anastasia is doing this, but how brave she is in the face of such betrayal. Being in Tyur'ma has made her tougher. I don't know whether to be proud or sad.

We sit quietly for a while. I think about Nicolai and his reluctance in the laundry room when we were about to escape. I think about everything the prince said, and then about him and his sister arguing on top of the wall at Tyur'ma. I see everything in a different light, and it makes sense. It fits together like clockwork.

But I don't understand all of it. Not yet.

"Who do you think started the fire?" I ask Sasha. I thought it could have been Nicolai I saw running from the tower that night. But it couldn't have been him if he works for the prince.

"We trust Katia and Feliks, don't we," she says, though it's not really a question. I do. Totally.

"Natalia, then," she says.

If Anatol had Nicolai inside Tyur'ma, then Anastasia could just as easily have had someone. Someone who would have kept close. I nod. "She could be a spy. Anastasia needed us to stay locked in Tyur'ma because we were the only ones who knew you hadn't stolen the music box. So she had Natalia steal the pick. Natalia had been watching me from the start. But then . . . she forced us to escape. I don't understand."

Sasha presses her lips together, her eyes fixed on the comforter. "Maybe her orders changed."

"To what? Why would she want us out of the prison?"

"So she could . . ." My sister answers before she thinks through to the end of the thought. She draws her knees up to her chest, elbows sticking out of the sleeves of her borrowed tunic. Misery is written all over her face. "I think Natalia was supposed to lead us somewhere the princess could capture us." Her eyes go wide. "I bet Anastasia had the warden put Natalia in my cell."

"We're safe," I say, tightening my arm around her shoulders. "I think Natalia ran away." I almost sent Sasha off with that spy to who knows what fate. I think about Feliks and Katia again. I wish I knew they were safe.

A cloud sweeps over part of the moon, dimming the light falling into the room.

"We should tell Anatol. Go to the queen," I say.

Sasha's shoulders are hunched under my arm. "Without proof, it would be our word against the future queen's. It's treason."

The word sinks cold and hard to the floor.

"We have to find proof, then," I say. "We have to find the music box."

❧

I wake a second time from a fitful sleep filled with broken dreams. Sasha is already up and by the door, poised with the silver hairbrush in her raised hand. There's a quiet, insistent knocking.

We exchange wide-eyed glances. I put my foot to the floor.

"Valor?" someone whispers on the other side. "Can I use this key?"

Sasha's hand wavers.

"Nicolai?" I ask.

"It's me. May I . . . come in?"

Sasha's quizzical face might be funny if this wasn't the second unexpected and confusing visitor to arrive in as many hours. But Nicolai's voice is polite to the point of timidity, and there's only one of him and two of us. Besides, I have a question or two for him, and I want to know why he's here.

I look to my sister and she nods her agreement, stepping

back from the door and silently returning the hairbrush to the dressing table.

"You may enter," I say, though it feels strange—it's not even my room.

A key slides into the lock. Nicolai pokes his head through first, then steps in quickly and closes the door. His dark hair is clean and neatly brushed.

He bites his lip. "I shouldn't be here."

"Then why are you?" I swing my other foot out of bed and stand. Sasha crosses her arms, and we both wait.

"I came to say I'm sorry. I'm not a traitor. Not really."

"What are you, then?" Sasha demands. "*Who* are you?" She looks him up and down. He's wearing a uniform with a sash, a bit like . . . the Guard.

Nicolai twists his hands together. "I'm still Nicolai. I was doing my duty—trying to help. The prince said I had to try to find out any information I could. He said it could save the whole realm." He looks down at the carpet. "Anyway, I just wanted to see you, to say sorry. I really have to go—"

"How did you even get into Tyur'ma?" I demand. "Did the warden know who you were?"

Nicolai shakes his head. "Prince Anatol told her I was a prisoner he had a very personal interest in—that I was an apprentice guard who had stolen a horse, but that I was to be shown some leniency. Warden Kirov takes her job very seriously—maybe too seriously—and once Prince Anatol explained that I could take a position of responsibility because of my training, she assured him his wishes would be followed."

"What training?" asks Sasha.

His shoulders slump, and he really looks miserable. "How do you think I felt? Signing up with the Guard for my apprenticeship and getting recruited in the first week to be some sort of spy instead?" He shakes his head. "I don't think I was cut out for it at all. I'm really not a good liar. Look, I have to get back to the barracks before they miss me," he says. "I really am sorry, Valor."

"You sneaked out by yourself? Did you *steal* the key?" I can feel a small smile trying to break through.

He gives a sheepish smile of his own. "Maybe I learned a thing or two from you." The smile disappears. "He's a good person, the prince. You can trust him."

Before I can answer, he ducks out of the door, and the lock clicks once more.

$\sim \sim \sim$

In the morning a knock wakes me. I slide out of bed and open the door. I stare at Prince Anatol, and he stares back. At first he looks uncertain, and then he simply holds out a tray. On it is a bowl of fruit, two glasses, a jug, and several bread rolls.

Sasha is still asleep, her arm thrown above her head, hair over her face. I stand aside, and the prince pushes the door closed with his boot. He's wearing a paler blue today, covered by a black cloak.

I take a roll and bite into it. Maybe I'll better be able to say what I'm about to say if I'm not distracted by my stomach. I have to tell the prince his sister's a liar and a thief. That she plotted against our queen and country and threw my sister's life away to do it.

And I have to say it, because I need to make an ally of him.

"I know it wasn't you who stole the music box," I tell him. "And I know why you haven't found out who did do it."

He stares at me.

I tried to think of some way to gild the truth all night, but there's really no way to do it, so I just come out with it.

"It's Anastasia."

I swallow and give him a moment to take in what I just said. I can't look at him. When he doesn't storm out of the room or call for the Guard or summon the queen, and when my heartbeat has stopped thudding in my ears, I say it again. Then I tell him what Sasha and I talked about last night.

Anatol's expression is grave. "This is treason," he says. "You can't expect me to believe it."

But I hear it—the note of uncertainty in his voice. It's like he doesn't want to believe it, but already did a little before I started talking.

"Think about it," I say. "You've been trying to find out who it was for weeks, and you couldn't. Why is that? Who else could it be?"

I try to explain what Sasha said about the princess and Pyots'k. I'm not sure I do as good a job as my sister could have done, but she's exhausted and sleeping, and I need to convince the prince so that when Sasha wakes I can tell her I'm going to prove her innocence and fix this whole sorry mess.

"I think it makes sense to you already, doesn't it?" I say quietly.

Anatol plunges his hands through his hair, his cloak falling back over his shoulders. He unclasps it irritably and flings it to the floor. "Nothing about this makes sense. She is my sister. Surely you, of all people, can understand how little I wish this to be true."

Sasha makes a noise behind us. When I turn, she's up, her face bright and alert, still creased from sleep. I didn't even hear her stir. "Wishing it not to be true is an entirely different thing from whether it is or not," she says gently.

I think she might have been awake the whole time I've been speaking, because she's talking to the prince but looking at me with a pride that makes me feel warm inside.

My sister gets up and takes an apple from the tray, but doesn't say anything further. Then she grabs a pillow from the bed, dropping it to the floor so she can sit on it. She pats the rug next to her.

I'm not sure if princes are used to sitting on floors, but I sit cross-legged on the thick rug and lean against one of the posts of the bed. Anatol joins us, resting his elbows on the knees of his crossed legs and locking his fingers together. He takes one of the rolls and tears a corner off it.

His expression is a lot like Sasha's when she's deep in thought, figuring out something difficult and not entirely pleasant. We eat quietly while he thinks, but eventually questions are bursting out of me. I have to prove my sister is innocent, or crawling through that tunnel and half drowning to escape will have been for nothing.

"Did you have Nicolai steal a metal pick from my cell?" I ask.

His brow furrows. "No. Do you know who started the fire in the tower?"

The prince sweeps his cloak around himself, and I drag the coverlet from the bed, throwing it around my and Sasha's shoulders. She tells him what we think about Natalia.

"At the prison, Anastasia nodded to a big, strong-looking girl," he says. "I wondered about it, but then we argued and I thought no more on it."

He rubs a hand across his brow, mussing his hair. "So my own sister had her spy light the fire in the tower. I only just got away into the tunnel." He looks at Sasha and bites his lip. "I'm sorry that she let you take the blame."

"You really believe me, then?" I ask.

I look him in the face. I thought his eyes were cold and haughty before, but now they're just hurt and tired. He *does* believe me. I even—*almost*—feel sorry for him.

We all know how important the music box is to the treaty with Magadanskya. Everything I care about—my country, my parents, my sister—is in the balance here. I have to get this right.

I lean forward. "We need to find the music box."

Anatol shakes his head. "I've searched the whole palace and haven't been able to find it. Your lives are at risk. Your *family's* lives are at risk. But I have to try to stop her. For the good of the realm. I just . . . I don't know what to do."

Sasha shivers. But having the prince on our side changes things. If he's willing to go against his own sister to do the right thing, then I'm willing to go as far as I need to in order to clear our names.

I shake my head. "You need to think bigger. Bolder."

"You have an idea?" A slow smile builds on his face. "This doesn't involve a crossbow, does it?"

"No." I smile back, but it soon fades. "Just a chance. A small one."

Princess Anastasia tore my family apart and blamed my innocent sister for her crime. There's no way I'm going to let her get away with it.

Prince Anatol looks straight into my eyes. "What do you have in mind?"

CHAPTER 21

Sasha and I change into the servants' uniforms the prince has borrowed for us, while he sits outside the marble bathroom, penning a note. "Are you sure this will work?" he asks through the door.

"Yes. Write it exactly as I said," I call out, slipping the embroidered tunic over the trousers I'm wearing.

"Valor!" Sasha whips her sash at me. "Shouldn't you be a little less bossy?"

"Nonsense. I'm being . . . assertive." I take the sash from her, wrap it up, and tie it in the fashion of a servant over her tunic. It's not a bad fit. No one will suspect it's not hers at first glance.

"There," I say, turning her to face the gilded looking glass. "Two palace servants."

"As long as we don't see anyone who happens to recognize

the two disgraced daughters of the queen's former first huntswoman and adviser," she says.

I put my hands on her shoulders. "Details," I say with a smile—though I couldn't eat the food the prince brought for us along with the uniforms. My stomach feels twisted the wrong way.

We hurry back into the bedroom, where the prince is sitting at the dresser, leaning over a scroll of paper. He adds a flourish to the end of the note, blots the ink, and offers it to me.

Dearest Anastasia,

My spies have gathered information regarding two girls that might be of interest to you. Meet me with all haste in the hothouse so that we may speak of the matter privately.

Your brother and humble servant,
Anatol

"It's perfect," I say.

He rolls it up and tucks it into his tunic.

"Ready?" I ask Sasha.

She smoothes down her braids and nods.

Prince Anatol opens the door, and we follow him back along the dull corridor and through the first secret panel to the second, where we all stand straining our ears. Silence.

He slides back the panel, and we slip out into the warmth and light of the gold-and-blue palace corridor. I keep my eyes lowered as I follow the prince, Sasha behind me. As we pass the hidden entrance to the dungeon, a chill creeps across my skin.

Prince Anatol strides up a grand sweeping staircase with a polished marble rail. The low hum of voices carries up the stairs. My blood rushes loud in my ear as we walk across the mezzanine. Below us on the mosaic-tiled floor, two courtiers are engaged in an argument. A group of the queen's advisers stands close together, their deep-blue cloaks blending like the petals of some great flower as they discuss matters of policy. Three servants wait quietly at the edges of the room in case they're needed.

Anatol stiffens and hesitates. We're going to have to walk right past them all to get to the hothouse. He takes a breath and leads us down another staircase. This one pools like the train of a wedding dress on the floor in front of the courtiers. They stop their argument and bow as soon as they see the prince. He inclines his head, and I dip into a low bow, keeping my head down, praying they don't notice my burning ears.

"Here, girl." One of the advisers holds her cloak out in my direction as we pass. I recognize her voice—she worked with my father. I stutter the beginning of an answer, stuck between not wanting to face her and not wanting to draw attention by ignoring her. My face is burning. Anatol flicks his hand, and one of the palace servants comes running across to take the cloak.

The prince leads on, and I hold my breath, expecting a hand to stop me or a voice to call out. But the invisibility of servants protects us, and we reach the glass doors of the hothouse. The ornate entrance of the palace, the same one I walked through in chains a few short weeks ago, is closed against the snowdrifts outside. I hope my friends are safe and warm. I hope Feliks knows somewhere in the city they can go. And that I'll get the chance to find out if they're okay later.

We step into hot, wet air. Deep green leaves as shiny as polished malachite press in on all sides.

"Come. This way," says Anatol. We push through the foliage, overgrown as it is onto the small paths.

"This is a good place for you to hide," he says. "I'll lead her here."

I sweep a thick tendril laden with bloodred blooms out of my way. A glass fountain stands in the middle of the room. Red, blue, and gold fish swim in its depths. Water sprays out of the mouth of a giant glass snow leopard rearing on its back legs in the middle of the fountain.

"Good. Go. We'll be well hidden," I tell the prince.

His throat bobs. He nods once, and then he's gone. He'll find a servant to deliver the note, then wait inside the entrance to the hothouse for the princess to arrive.

Sasha is already pushing through the dense vines to find a place to hide. "Here," she says after a minute.

Bright-smelling leaves brush my hands and face as I follow her into a hollow where the plants tangle above us. I peer out at the fountain, arranging a few big fronds so that we're hidden. Sasha's shoulder bumps mine. "I can't believe we're doing this," she whispers.

I can't believe it either.

She presses her lips together, but it's obvious she's just trying to be brave. I was angry, even a bit upset, when I thought Nicolai had betrayed us. How much worse it is that the princess has used her so.

The door creaks slightly. We both hold perfectly still. I catch a glimpse of Anatol's anxious face, and then he disappears again. We wait. As my legs stiffen, I become sure that it won't work. Anastasia isn't coming.

I see Anatol again. He's pacing in the little space by the door.

The door opens. Anatol says something in a low voice. The voice gets louder, plants and leaves swish, and he walks out right in front of the fountain. His eyes dart about but land on nothing. He can't see us.

"Must we go so far into this place? You know how I hate it."

I take shallow breaths. Anastasia.

"I am sorry, sister. I thought you would rather talk about this away from prying eyes and ears. We can go elsewhere if it pleases you."

The princess, upright in the tight bodice of her white dress, sweeps forward and glances down at the fish in the fountain, disdain curling her lip. Pearls adorn the diamond headdress that holds her piled braids back, and on each of her eyelashes sits a tiny white pearl to match.

"No. You may tell me what you have to tell me here. What have your spies uncovered?"

Prince Anatol holds his hands behind his back. "That the girls have escaped from Tyur'ma—"

The princess stamps her foot. "I know this. Why do you waste my time?"

"Then you know that they are still out there in the city, free to tell their story of innocence to whoever will listen."

There's a pause.

"Innocence?" asks the princess. "Whatever do you mean?"

My heart beats fast and hard. Sasha grips my hand so tight it hurts.

I think Anatol is going to have to accuse her outright, but brother and sister must know each other as well as Sasha and I do. The looks passing between them say it all.

Anastasia laughs, her dark hair shining in the light pouring in through the glass roof. A dark ruby the size of a date glints on her finger. "And who will believe the words of two vengeful criminals from a disgraced family over those of the future queen?"

I crouch, as still as an ice sculpture. Sasha is silent beside me, but I'm sure she feels sicker than I do to hear her employer, her *friend*, talk about our family like that.

"No one will believe them," says Anatol. "Which is why they intend to break into the palace and find the music box."

The princess laughs, but it fades quickly. "Let them try," she says.

"It's unlikely that they could get in, of course; I agree." Anatol sits on the side of the fountain and trails his fingers in the water. "Even for girls who evaded Warden Kirov and escaped Tyur'ma. You are right, as always, sister. Still, I hear that they are the first to escape in over three hundred years. And despite the best efforts of our guards, we have yet to find one member of their group."

Anastasia's mouth is a pink slash in her delicate face. "Why do you come to me with this now, dear brother? Do you wish to ally with me over Mother? Even at the expense of Valor and her precious sister?"

The prince shrugs elegantly. "I have no wish to see innocent people locked up. But I also have no wish to further displease my future queen." He drops to his knees in front of her and kisses her hand, his dark curls bent over the ruby on her finger.

A scuffle in the leaves by my right ear makes me jerk. Wings scrabble on leaves and a blur of yellow flashes past, tweeting in fright. Sasha lets out a squeak and bites her lip. My heart beats and beats with the bird's wings as it flits up into the canopy above.

"Just a bird," says Anatol, who has leapt to his feet. "But we've dallied here long enough. May I trust that bringing this information to you proves my loyalty?"

The princess's lips curve into a smile, but her eyes are cold. "You may."

I don't believe a word.

"Then I'll take my leave." He hurries away, and moments later the glass doors open and close.

I barely breathe, studying the princess. Unaware that she's not alone, she stares into the fountain, her hands twisting in front of her.

Take the bait, I think to myself, over and over.

And like a winter hare in one of my snares, she does.

The princess turns on her heel and runs for the hothouse doors. Sasha lets out a breath and surges forward, but I hold her back, a finger pressed to my lips. I know how to hunt.

I slip through the foliage, not letting it brush my tunic. The soft leather of my servants' shoes, designed not to mark the beautiful floors of the palace, is silent on the tile path. The princess pauses at the doors, pulls herself up straight, and swings the doors open. She turns left. We wait for three agonizing seconds, and then follow her.

The great hall is empty. I peek around the corner. A long corridor leads to a large gallery with a high-arched golden door at the end of it. Anastasia's dress flares out as she pushes the door open, glances behind, and tears forward.

We run after her. I keep Sasha to the side of the corridor, ready to hide behind the thick drapes framing every window if the princess pauses. I signal to her to keep her eyes open, covering our backs.

When we reach the gallery, we have to run out into the open through a room with a domed ceiling painted to look like a blue summer sky. The light and shade on the wispy clouds is so real that I pause for the tiniest amount of time. I peer around one golden door. Anastasia's gone.

Panic makes me bold and I rush out, followed by Sasha, into the corridor beyond.

"Watch yourself, girl!" An elderly woman wearing eyeglasses and clutching a pile of scrolls in her creased hands frowns down at me.

I open my mouth, but nothing comes out.

"Begging your pardon," says Sasha, ducking her head and pulling me into a bow.

I raise my head a little and see a glimpse of white disappearing around a corner ahead.

"I should think so," says the woman, who continues on her way, muttering to herself.

We look at each other and then fly down the hallway, but it ends in a tall tapestry of a bird's-eye view of the city. No more turns, no more doors.

I throw my hands up into my hair. "I thought I saw her dress."

Sasha spins around in a circle. She presses her lips together, deep in thought, then starts pulling and pressing at the panels around us. I help, all the time glancing down the length of the hallway, but though my fingers are desperate and I tear a nail, nothing moves.

"Are you sure you saw her?" Sasha is breathing hard, trying not to panic.

"I—I did. I thought I did."

I turn around once more. "She can't have disappeared. She must have gone somewhere." I grab the tapestry, dragging the heavy material away from the wall. The panels behind it are dark wood, like the ones that lead to the other secret corridors. But still we can't make anything move.

"Look," says Sasha. She points at the palace on the city plan. The embroidery on the tapestry is black for the whole city, apart from the palace, which is copied in the bright colors of its onion domes. "I've heard Father mention this before, but I didn't know where they were. You know the palace has . . ." She reaches up and presses the embroidery of the palace. A shifting sound comes from behind the tapestry. I smile, hope springing back up.

"Secret passageways," she finishes.

When we lift the tapestry of the city this time, there's a narrow corridor, dusty from lack of use. We hurry forward, keeping one hand to the wall. The air is thick and musty, and I stifle a sneeze. A scuffling sound comes from below us. Sasha clutches my arm, and we creep forward until we come to a flight of narrow wooden stairs.

Low light bleeds up them, leaving us in shadow at the top. I put my foot out onto the top step. It creaks when I lean my weight on it. I freeze, then pull back and try the second step down. It's silent, so I sneak on and Sasha follows, stepping where I step.

Halfway down, the steps twist. We can't go on without the risk of being seen. I crouch and peer into the murky half light. A small room opens out before me. At the far end is a door in dark shadow. The princess stands with her back to me, the hem of her white dress dusted with cobwebs.

I draw back against the step, barely breathing, and bring my face in close to Sasha's ear. "Fetch Anatol and the queen. Bring them here. Run." She slips away into the shadows, back to meet Anatol at the appointed place, leaving me to watch Anastasia. She's kneeling in front of an open chest.

She reaches into the chest and slowly lifts something from it. I grip the step so hard it hurts. It's the music box.

I've never seen anything so beautiful. The bottom is octagonal, burnished gold with etched filigree covering its surface. A golden key with tiny gold bows sticks out of the front. Sitting atop the base of the box is an egg, polished such a brilliant red that it almost glows. It's studded down the center from top to bottom with diamonds that look pink. The music box has been right here in the palace in this dusty, dark room all along.

Anastasia looks over her shoulder, and I pinch my arms into my sides, trying to make myself as small as possible. I'm hidden in the shadows. She doesn't see me. Instead, she rubs her thumb and fingers together and turns the key in the music box. The mechanism inside clicks as the key turns, and when she releases it, the egg twirls in a slow circle. It splits apart along the seam of diamonds as it spins. A tinkling clockwork tune plays slowly, filling the small space, and I sit, transfixed. It sounds like tiny bells made of ice are ringing the sweetest tune.

Inside, the egg is polished gold. A tiny *matryoshka* doll rises from the center, spinning in the opposite direction of the egg. I lean forward, and the step my feet rest on groans.

Anastasia's head whips to the side. Her eyes wander as she listens. I draw back against the step, barely breathing. She pushes the little doll down, snaps the egg back together, and places the music box in the chest.

It's still dark behind me. No sign of Sasha. My pulse pounds in my throat. The princess dusts down her dress and gathers her skirts, heading for the steps.

I leap to my feet with one last desperate glance at the tapestry.

Anastasia gasps as the movement catches her attention, but almost instantly her expression flits to anger. My face is hidden in shadow. All she can see is the embroidered tunic. "How dare you follow me here? I shall have your position." She holds her head up, indignant.

"You shall have nothing at all," I say. "I am not your servant."

I place my hand on the stone wall to stop it from shaking and move down the steps into the light.

Her face changes with recognition, flashing with fear for a second. She clenches her jaw and regains her composure. "What is the meaning of this?" cries the princess, trying to step past me. "You escape from Tyur'ma only to come here?"

I block her way.

"So my pitiful brother was right. You still intend to prove your sister's innocence. Much good it will do you when you're arrested again and thrown in the dungeon. I don't think we'll be so lenient as to send you to Tyur'ma this time."

"You won't be able to send me anywhere once the queen finds out what you've done," I say.

She smiles an arrogant, triumphant smile. "My mother will never believe you." I clench my jaw tight as she laughs. "'Mother, this unbalanced criminal broke into the palace and forced me to the hiding place where her thieving sister had hidden the music box.'" She clasps her hands over her heart dramatically. "'I was so frightened, Mother.'"

"My sister. Is not. A thief." I stand rigid on the stairs.

The princess takes a step back, narrowing her eyes. "Oh, but she *is*. Maybe she stole even more than the music box. Maybe I was just too kindhearted to say so at her trial. Of course, I'll have to admit it all now that you've come back to steal the music box again and attack me while doing it. I'll tell Mother and anyone else who cares to listen how it was just a pastry at first. Then a silver hairbrush or a gold locket. But that wasn't enough for Sasha, was it? No, she had her eye on the music box. She's always been a thief. A nasty little thief."

I take a step into the room, my hands clenched at my sides. "She's not, and you know it. I know you framed her. Anatol knows, and he's—"

"*Anatol?* His name is *Anatol* now, is it? Not His Royal Highness? How nice for you. I hope you'll all be very happy together when my mother banishes you. Or maybe she'll decide to do something much worse to you and Sasha."

My cheeks burn. I try not to let my anger loose, but it flares like the fire in the tower. "You could have killed your own brother. If he'd been in the tower when you had your spy burn it down, he'd be dead."

"And if Natalia weren't so useless, she would have brought your sister with her after you made your silly escape, and Sasha would be gone by now, and I wouldn't have to deal with this tiresome mess."

I'm so angry that I can't stop the words from spilling out of my mouth. "How could you do that to Sasha? Why did it have to be her? She *loved* you."

"Yes, and she *loved* my mother too. And Mother *loved* her. All she has to do is ask, and the queen of Demidova says yes. Not to her own daughter, of course. I'm only the girl who will run this country. *I* can't be trusted to make decisions by myself. But *Sasha?* Sasha's so wonderful, Sasha's such a quick study, Sasha will make such a brilliant adviser. We won't have to worry when Anastasia is on throne, because *Sasha*—"

"Don't talk about her like that," I shout. "Don't you dare even say her name!"

Anastasia draws herself up to her full height and leans into my face. "Her name will be worth nothing when I'm finished. You really should have stayed in Tyur'ma, Valor, because you are going to beg to go back there before today is over. Get out of my way." She waves her hand imperiously in my face.

I stand my ground. "No."

"You dare to defy me?" Her eyes flash, her nostrils flare, and then she brings back her hand. My fist clenches.

"Stop."

It's only one word, but the command is absolute. I spin around with my fist still clenched.

Queen Ana stands halfway down the steps.

CHAPTER 22

My hands drop to my sides.

The queen glides down the steps in a gown that sweeps the floor, a white wrap over her shoulders, diamonds and pearls at her throat and on her headdress. Her presence fills the tiny, dimly lit room. Prince Anatol appears behind her, his hair rumpled. Sasha is at his side, out of breath, her face flushed.

Princess Anastasia glares at me, her headdress askew, braids spilling down onto her shoulders. She straightens her dress and stands side by side with her mother. The two of them regard me, the queen with an unreadable expression, the princess with gleeful malice. I've done exactly what she wanted. And ruined everything.

I make a clumsy bow to the queen, though it's more of a slump than anything else. "Anatol, fetch my personal guards," says the queen.

He opens his mouth to say something, but she turns her gaze on him and he bows and leaves.

The queen takes a deep breath, holding her hands gracefully in front of her. She looks down at Sasha, who has her tunic clenched in her hands. "Where is the music box?"

Sasha clears her throat, her gaze flitting to me. "I—I don't know, Your Majesty."

Princess Anastasia makes an outraged gasp. "Surely you don't intend to continue this charade any further? Mother, these *criminals*—"

Queen Ana silences her daughter with one look, though when she turns away, the princess stares resentment at her through narrowed eyes.

"It's here," I say, stepping forward and swinging open the chest. "But, begging your pardon, Your Majesty, if you'll permit me, I can explain everything. I—"

"Must we listen to these lies?" cries the princess. "This girl *attacked* me. Her sister is a thief, and she tried to kill Anatol."

"Silence, Anastasia." The ferocity in the queen's voice makes me jump. "I heard every word you said not five minutes ago as this *girl* stood here and faced you in order to save her sister from an unjust fate and restore her family's honor."

The princess breathes hard, pink blotches rising up her neck and spreading across her face. "It was all lies, Mother.

I was trying to provoke a confession from her. This one"—
she points a shaking finger at Sasha—"is a thief and a liar.
They're plotting against me. Anatol too. It's treason to plot
against the queen."

"But you are not the queen," says Anatol, now returned
with two guards who wear white sashes.

The queen smiles at him, sadness in her eyes. "No,
she is not. And nor will she ever be." She nods to the guards
as though a great weight is upon her, and as they move
to stand on either side of Anastasia, she looks at her
daughter. "You are right. It *is* treason to plot against the
queen."

My sister stands, her hands still clenched in her servants' tunic, her eyes glistening with tears. I want to make
it all better, but I know I can't, and I daren't move.

"More than that," the queen continues, her voice dip-
ping, "think what you have done to this family—a family
who served us well for many years. And for what?"

The defiance on the princess's face shifts to desperation. "I saved their lives!" She looks at me. "Who do you
think ordered that fire lit? You'd have died in that ice
dome if it wasn't for me. I would never have left Sasha in
there."

I open my mouth to tell her exactly what I think of what
she's done, but the queen speaks first.

"If what Anatol tells me about your plans to ally

Demidova with Pyots'k is true, then you have placed us all in grave danger. Can you not see that, Anastasia? Allowing them to launch their warships from our ports benefits us only in the short term. What is the point in us being rich with their gold if they lose their war and a returning army from across the sea attacks us?"

The princess looks like a hunted animal, cornered and furious, feral in her anger. "Even now," she says, her eyes flashing at Sasha, "you take *her* side over mine."

"*Especially* now I take her side over yours," says the queen. "You are in the wrong!"

The princess's jaw is clamped tight, her lips pressed together so hard they're white.

"Have you nothing more to say, Anastasia?" It's painful to hear the queen's voice, beseeching, angry, heartbroken. "Tell me what you have done."

We all wait for an answer, but none comes.

The queen presses her hands together and pulls herself up straight with a visible effort. "If you won't speak to me, you will be questioned like any other prisoner. I *will* know what you have agreed to and what plans may already be in place." She turns to her guards. "Take her to the dungeon. Perhaps a little time alone will allow her to think about what she wishes to say."

Sasha and I lock eyes as the princess is escorted from the dusty room and silence descends.

Slowly, I walk toward the chest, open the lid, and carefully lift out the music box. Its solid weight rests in my hands. It really is breathtaking—the colors so vivid, the detail so intricate. When I turn around, the queen stands, Anatol on one side, Sasha on the other.

I step forward and offer the music box to Queen Ana.

CHAPTER 23

I sit on the palace steps outside the great doors, looking across the gardens. Sasha sits on my left, Anatol on my right, his uniform and the sword at his side keeping him rigid. I pull my furs closer. The sky is white, the onion domes of the palace towering at our backs. The cobbled square beyond the gardens is filling up quickly. Queen Ana wasted no time in getting word to Lady Olegevna that the music box had been found, and only the morning after the confrontation in the secret room, the queen is keen to show her people that the treaty *can* be signed after all.

The new ceremony won't have the ice sculptures the first one had—there's no time to replicate them—but it will feature something much more important: the music box finally being returned to its rightful owner, and the alliance between Demidova and Magadanskya completed at last.

"Do you think your friends will come forward?" asks the prince. His hair has been slicked down, but already a curl at the front is threatening to break free. Notices have been put up around the city that Katia and Feliks are to be interviewed and possibly pardoned as part of the queen's investigation into the running of Tyur'ma. Prince Anatol is heading the commission. Sasha can't wait to tell Father that the reform he wanted is happening at last.

I smile. "Katia, maybe. Feliks? I don't know." Beyond the golden gates at the end of the palace gardens, across the cobbled square, a thriving market bustles once again with vendors hawking their wares. Smells of roasted chestnut and hot chocolate and baked potato mingle in the air. The noises and scents carry faintly to the three of us. I imagine Feliks, his pockets filled with stolen dates, grinning as he slips through the crowd.

"How is the queen?" I ask Anatol. I haven't seen her since she pardoned us and sent for our parents to reinstate them as first huntswoman and adviser. She's been busy organizing the events planned for today. "And the king?"

Anatol smiles in the same sad way his mother did yesterday in the secret room. "Their hearts are heavy, even though the realm will be safe once the peace treaty is signed. Mother says she will continue to rule for now. Maybe until I have a daughter who can take the crown."

He blushes bright red, and I study the veins in the marble step at my feet.

"Valor." Sasha taps my arm, rising to her feet.

I stand too, joy pushing me up onto the tips of my toes to see better. At the edge of the market, two figures break into the cobbled square: a woman in gray furs and a man in a deep-blue cloak. They hurry across the square, making their way through the rapidly swelling crowd to the golden gates, where two of the Guard wait to admit them.

I look down at Anatol, and he smiles. "Go."

I take Sasha's hand and we run to meet our parents, our boots creaking on the new snow. My mother's arms are already outstretched, her face bright and joyful and anguished and relieved all at once. She doesn't know which one of us to look at first, but she's drinking us both in with her eyes.

We're pulled forward like two magnets to our parents, and then they both have their arms around us, the four of us locked tightly together, Father sobbing into my hair. I'm still holding on for all I'm worth when the music starts. It's a grand marching band of brass instruments and drums out in the square, organized to announce the beginning of the new ceremony. We must take our places, but as we move to the side of the gates to await the queen, we link hands, Sasha and I between our parents. I look up at my mother.

She shakes her head in wonder, though her eyes shine with tears. "I am so proud of you, Valor."

My throat goes tight and I can't speak, but then the queen makes her appearance on the palace steps, Anatol and his father behind her. She leads a procession flanked by Guards, with four servants following Anatol, each carrying the handled corner of a glass case draped in gold cloth.

As the queen reaches us at the gates, her eyes land on me. She smiles, but something flits across her face—a fast-moving storm cloud. I move to her left side in a place of honor, as I've been instructed. Sasha takes her own place on the queen's other side, and my parents step in behind the king and Prince Anatol.

Lady Olegevna awaits us at the fountain on horseback, as she did what seems like years ago now, to complete the peace treaty. I can't help but glance at the tower I shot my crossbow from. The turret has been boarded up. I look to the queen. We keep moving, the crowd cheering as we approach the fountain, and Queen Ana speaks in a low voice without turning her head.

"Girls, there's something I must tell you. I thought you should be the first to know."

Her strained tone makes my heart kick up its pace.

"I received word minutes ago that Princess Anastasia is no longer in the dungeon."

My sister draws in a sharp breath.

I'm just as shocked as she is. "I—I don't— Where is she?"

We step up onto the wide stone rim of the fountain, the rear legs of the magnificent stone horse rising in front of me.

The queen shakes her head. "I do not know where or how it happened, or what she intends to do. But somehow, she has escaped without a trace."

My stomach lurches, and I try to catch Sasha's eye. But we've reached the far side of the fountain, the music has stopped, and the crowds are quieting for the queen to speak. I hardly hear what she says. Lady Olegevna's horse's hooves click on the cobbles as she dismounts and joins us on the fountain.

I look out across the crowd, scanning faces, and have to stop myself from making a little surprised noise. Two figures, cloaked, with hoods pulled down low, stand near the market. A boy grins at me, two large front teeth visible even at a distance. The end of a pale braid sticks out from under the hood of the taller figure. Feliks and Katia. But they'll be pardoned, I'm sure of it. Why haven't they come forward? Haven't they seen the signs around the city?

Then Katia shakes her head. Slowly. Deliberately. She puts a finger to her lips. Our eyes lock, and her expression is so grave that I want to run to her, ask her why.

The queen has finished her speech. She and Lady Olegevna are now standing together with the glass case between them. A huge gasp from the crowd pulls my gaze away from Katia. Sasha has tugged free the gold cloth covering the case with a flourish, and everyone can see the music box.

Prince Anatol steps forward to me, saying in a low voice, "You're quite certain you don't have a crossbow about you?"

I manage a smile over my shoulder. He doesn't yet know about his sister. And he deserves to have this moment. Just like Sasha does. I watch her as she opens the glass case and takes the music box in her hands. I see the nervous glance she darts at the queen and the reassuring nod Queen Ana returns.

My sister turns to Lady Olegevna, and her voice rings out over the hushed square.

"On behalf of Queen Ana of Demidova, please accept the return of this treasure belonging rightfully to the realm of Magadanskya. It brings with it a much-needed, productive, and prosperous alliance—one that we all deeply hope will stand the test of time."

Sasha and I argued back and forth over who should deliver this speech, who should have the honor of handing over the music box. She said I should have it, and listed more reasons than I could comfortably listen to as to why. I was less eloquent, but equally determined. And listening to her now, as she offers the music box to Lady Olegevna and the crowd breaks out into cheers and rapturous applause, the queen smiling, her face clear of all worry for a moment, I know I was right to insist.

Nobody could have done this but Sasha.

ACKNOWLEDGMENTS

This book wouldn't be in your hands without the hard work and love of a lot of people, but there are three in particular to whom I owe a giant amount of gratitude.

My agent, Andrea Somberg, who is endlessly positive and helpful, who literally made my dreams come true, and who I swear never sleeps because how else could she always be around to answer every e-mail I've ever sent right away?

My editor, Hali Baumstein. I can't quantify how much better this book is after she sprinkled her enthusiasm and insight over the snow in Demidova. I struck gold when she decided she liked this story.

My friend and critique partner, Michelle Krys. This book would be a pile of comma splices and this author would be lost if she wasn't there to read every word I write.

Thank you also to the teams at Bloomsbury in the US and the UK, particularly to Cindy Loh, Sally Morgridge, Ilana Worrell, and Ben Holmes (I'm so sorry about the speech marks!), and to Colleen Andrews and Donna Mark who designed the beautiful cover and interior. I hope my words do their hard work and Torstein Nordstrand's gorgeous art justice.

To my friends Amy Tintera, Amy Christine Parker, Corinne Duyvis, Deborah Hewitt, Gemma Cooper, Kim Welchons, Lori M. Lee, Natalie C. Parker, and Stephanie Winkelhake. They write the best books and give the best advice.

To Julia Churchill: thank you. I learned a lot.

I've met a lot of kind and talented people online. Thank you for your time and help, Jennifer Honeybourn, Katie Zachariou, Emma Madden, Kate Kelly, Kathleen Nelson, JD Field, Mark Stone, Chris Kinkaid, and Linda McLaren.

To cool teachers Mrs. Blakemore and Mr. Ryan: thank you. You'll be pleased to hear I'm not incapable of speech, I did care, and I was listening.

To Dad, for letting me take all the library books on his ticket when I maxed out my own, and to all my family. Dave, Dan, Tom, Leo, Sam, and Elysia: I love you; thanks for being mine.